Lynx

The Cursed Series

By

LM Evans

Copyright

CONTENTS

DEDICATION

This book is dedicated to my Nan and Grampa,

my guardian Angel's.

Two soulmates united again in the stars.

I will always love you both xx

Acknowledgements

To my husband and children, I love you all. Thank you for letting me follow a dream and to do what I thought was never possible.

Thank you to my parents, for making sure I kept up with my schoolwork when I was younger. To my sisters, family, and friends for supporting and believing in me, I love you all.

Being an indie author is scary, there can be dark sides but also lots of good. If you are lucky enough to surround yourself with amazing people, then you are truly blessed. I have made so many friends along the way since I began this journey. To those who started this crazy train with me and those who have hopped on board since, I couldn't do this without your support, it means so much.

So, I want to say thank you to Debbie Williams, Mia Hudson, Diane Lewis, Christine Lewis, Beth Jones, Nicola Yates, M. A. Foster, Sienna Grant, Scarlet Le Clair, Emma Lloyd, Leanne Colvin, Keira Garbett,

I also want to say a massive thank you to my two awesome editors, Juliet Driscoll and Maria Lazarou Who are bloody amazing.

To my Cover Designer and formatter Maria Lazarou at Obsessed by Books. I don't know where I would be without you.

Lastly, I want to say a massive thank you to all the bloggers who helped spread the word about my work.

Author Message

Readers, in this book I mention the animal wall. This is an actual place, although this book is fiction. The animal wall is real.

It runs along the walls on the outside of Cardiff Castle, in South Wales, UK. It consists of fifteen animals made from stone. One of the original animals was meant to be a seahorse but the idea of it was dismissed. One of the animals is an actual Lynx, which inspired my story.

I hope you enjoy this as much as I did writing it. If you do, please leave a review on Amazon. If you find yourself in the Welsh capital, then go check them out.

Quote

My eyes are tempted by the smile of an angel, and your lips whisper secrets of forbidden love

Unknown

Blurb

A year later, on the anniversary of her parent's death, Eliana isn't coping, the devastating pain is still so raw.

Seeking solace, she visits her Mother's favourite place; the public gardens of a local Castle. Deep in her memories, she's brought back to the present by a voice in the dark telling her to leave.

The gardens though, give her comfort, so Eliana finds herself returning. Again, as night falls the mysterious voice tells her to leave. Feeling no danger from the strange voice, she continues her visits, until one night the source of the voice is suddenly revealed.

After her first visit to the gardens, feeling stronger, she goes to the spare room and starts going through her parent's belongings. Something she's put off this whole year. She finds a wooden box, she's not seen before. Opening the box, the contents leave her confused as to what she finds.

What secrets does the box hold?

Who is the voice that keeps telling Eliana to leave the Castle Garden

CHAPTER ONE

I can't believe it's been a year since my parents died in a car crash. Today, the anniversary of their death, both my aunts have phoned to see how I am coping. I tell them I'm doing okay, but it hasn't got any easier as the time has gone by.

Today, I find myself here at their graveside. I bend down to place red roses in a vase on their grave. There is a photo of my parents on their wedding day on the black heart headstone, with gold writing that says:

IN LOVING MEMORY OF
NATASHA AND MATHEW STEVENS.
BELOVED MOTHER AND FATHER
DIED 24TH FEBRUARY 2019

It hurts like hell to come to the cemetery, knowing they aren't here anymore. The only peace I have now, is knowing mum and dad are together again at least. Kneeling on the grass beside the grave, I lean over and touch the photo on the gravestone.

"I miss you both so much. I wish you were here. I wish you could send me a sign to tell me everything is going to be okay. I know I have Aunt Lucy and Aunt Beth, but it's not the same. I will always love you both," I say as the tears fall.

I stay for a while, just talking to them, before heading off. The thought of going back home, alone to an empty house, today of all days, doesn't appeal to me right now. So I decide to go into town and take a walk around to distract myself for a while.

THE daylight is fading as I walk around Cardiff. I find myself walking in and out of different shops. The city centre is getting quieter, the darker the sky gets. I walk up the high street and cross the road, before walking in front of Cardiff Castle.

Slowing my pace, I gaze at the different animals on the walls, that are on the outer parts of the castle. As I walk by and pause for a moment to take a closer look at a stone animal. It's a Lynx. I remember the stories my mother used to tell me about the animals coming alive at night. When I was younger, I believed her but as I grew up, I realised the stories weren't real.

How could they be?

The animals were made of stone and I notice the side gate to the castle gardens is closed. I glance around, before climbing over the gate and jump down to the other side. It's now pitch black but I still don't want to go home to an empty house. My parent's house. The darkness of the gardens doesn't scare me, even though the further I walk into the gardens, the more the sound of late night traffic and people fades. I turn on the torch that's on my phone and quickly flash it about to see if there is a bench. I finally see one a few feet away and walk slowly over to it and sit down. I turn off my torch, then I lie down on the bench and gaze into the night sky and listen to the traffic in the distance. I love the night sounds. Darkness surrounds me and I'm alone, just me in the castle gardens and a few stars in the night sky.

"You shouldn't be in here!"

A deep male voice shouts and makes me jump. I sit up.

I take a glance around, but it's too dark to see anything.

"Listen, pal, I'm not doing any harm. I've had a rough day, so leave me alone and mind your own business."

I sound braver than I feel, but I lie back down on the bench.

"You need to leave now," the voice shouts again, louder this time.

I sit up, before standing, then glance around to try and see who the voice belongs to, but there is no-one in sight.

"Okay, pal. I don't know who you are and since you won't show your face and you are hiding in the shadows like a coward, I am just going to ignore you."

Silence.

"Unless you want to show your face?"

I pause for a few moments, but still no reply.

"I'll take that as a no?"

Just then my phone starts to ring, and it's aunt Beth.

"Hello Aunt Beth"

"Hey sweetie how are you, did you go to the cemetery?"

"Yeah, I'm okay. I went to the cemetery and took some red roses to put on the grave."

"Did you stay long?"

"Yeah, I stayed for a bit, then jumped on a bus into town before going for a walk."

"Oh sweetie, you know I'm here for you. If you like, you can come and stay with me anytime, instead of being in that house on your own."

"I know Aunt Beth and thank you, but I think it's time to start sorting through some of the boxes in the house."

"Are you sure you're ready to do that, Eliana? Do you want me and Lucy to come over to help you?"

"Thanks but I can do this. You and Aunt Lucy sorted all the legal stuff out for me, which I'm grateful for, but this is something I need to do."

"Okay, sweetie, but if you do need us or have any questions, you know you can give us a ring, and we will come straight over."

"Thanks aunt Beth, I'd better go. I'll give you a ring after I sorted through those boxes in the spare room."

I hang up and swipe across my phone to turn my torch on. I flash it around the gardens to find whoever it was that told me to leave. The loud rustling of the bushes makes me spin around. My phone flies out of my hands, landing on the grass just behind me.

"I told you to leave if you don't you will regret ever coming in here," the voice shouts again.

"Fine, I'm going anyway, but I will definitely come back and keep coming back and you can't stop me," I shout back before walking over to my phone on the ground.

The torch, still on, highlights where it is on the ground. I pick it up before I walk back towards the gate. I climb over and take one look back in the gardens, before I make my way home.

CHAPTER TWO

I awake to the sound of knocking on the front door. I push back the duvet and rush out of the bedroom, down the stairs and unlock the door before opening it.

"Morning sleepy head."

It's my Aunt Lucy.

"Morning. What are you doing here?"

"Well, my darling Eliana, I am not just your father's sister but also your godmother. I also spoke to Beth yesterday, and she told me that you were planning on sorting through your parent's boxes today. So, here I am to help you, and no I will not leave you to do it on your own. So you can go get dressed and I shall put the kettle on," she explains all this before kissing me on the cheek, then closes the front door.

Not taking no for an answer, she walks off into the kitchen. I shake my head. She's stubborn but has a big heart.

"Shan't be long," I shout as I run back upstairs to get dressed.

I throw on a pair of black leggings, a white tank top and grab my phone and charger from beside my bed, before I head back downstairs. Lucy is standing on the top of the stairs holding two mugs of tea.

"Come on then, lead the way," she orders.

"I was going to come downstairs for a while."

"Eliana, I meant it when I said I am here to help you."

I take the cup of tea she's holding out.

"Thanks. I really appreciate you being here."

I walk across the landing, past my parent's room before stopping outside the spare room. Lucy squeezes my shoulder to let me know she's here for me. I push the handle down with my hand still holding my phone and charger and push the door open. Lots of cardboard boxes are stacked against the far wall. Walking into the room, I place my phone, charger and cup of tea on the windowsill. Lucy places her bag and cup of tea in the corner, before lifting a box off the stack. She places the box on the floor, before grabbing another to place on the floor next to the first box. She sits on the floor and I plop myself beside her, where we both open the boxes and start rummaging through them.

TWO hours later, and we are still going through the boxes, sorting stuff into piles. As I get to a third box, I come across this small wooden box with a lid that slides out.

"Oh, what's that?" Lucy asks.

I shrug.

"I don't know. I've never seen it before."

As I slide the lid off, I notice a pile of letters addressed to my dad, and open the one on top.

Dear Andrew,

If you are reading this letter, then it means I have died. Upon my death, I gave my lawyer instructions to send this letter to you.

You were my first love but sadly I was not yours. You fell into the arms of another woman, while you worked away. While you moved on leaving me heartbroken, you left a part of you with me. A son, Brent. I know you have moved on with your life and are now

married with a young daughter. Though my heart has never healed and it hurts knowing you moved on, I think you should get to know him. You should be the father Brent needs in his life. You can contact the lawyer who has his details. If you don't want anything to do with him, I beg you, please let your daughter know she has a big brother.

Love Lisa.

I glance over at Lucy.

"Did you know about this?" I ask.

She shakes her head.

"I swear to you Eliana, I am as shocked as you. Is there a photo of this Brent?"

I pass the letter to her and look through the rest of the envelopes. There is some more legal stuff for him, including his birth certificate which seems to be updated, as well as DNA results. At the bottom of the box, there is a small pile of photos of a baby boy. I look at each photo and pass them one by one to Lucy. Finally, I come to the last photo of a boy with blond, wearing a black T-shirt and jeans. He's smiling and she gazes at the photo.

"Oh my. It's like looking at Andy when he was younger," she cries, referring to dad's nickname.

A note is all that's left in the box, I pick it up and unfold it. It's a letter from Brent to dad.

Andrew,

I know mum sent you a letter explaining about me, but I want nothing to do with you. I am twenty-five and certainly don't need a sperm donor father in my life. I know you have a daughter and if she wants to meet me, I won't stop her, but as far as we are concerned you and I are nothing to each other.

Brent Carmichael

"I think I need to get out of here. Can we go for a walk or something?" I ask Lucy.

"Sure. Where would you like to go?"

"Anywhere, I need to get out of this house."

I grab my phone and rush out of the room to my bedroom and put on a pair of socks and trainers. I snatch my purse and keys from the dresser, before I run down the stairs. I take my pink hoodie from the bannister, just as Lucy comes downstairs with her bag and the two cups. She walks into the kitchen before placing them in the sink.

"Come on Eliana, let's go get some fresh air," she calls, and we leave through the front door. We head over to Roath Park in silence, until I have to ask the inevitable question.

"Aunt Lucy, did dad cheat on mum?"

"I really don't know, sweetie. He always seemed so happy with your mother. I have never heard of Lisa until now and definitely don't remember your dad ever talking about her."

"So, you think he may have met this Lisa, before he met mum?"

"Honestly, I don't know."

We walk in silence again until she asks the unavoidable question.

"What are you going to do about Brent? Do you want to meet him?"

"I don't know. I think I just need to figure things out in my head and not rush things."

"I understand. Well you haven't had breakfast yet and as it's nearly eleven-thirty, I'm taking you into town for some lunch. I'm going to arrange for Beth to meet us," she says, pressing the keypad on her phone.

We jump into her car, and she drives from Roath Park into the town centre. She parks the car in a car park, and we head to meet up with Aunt Beth.

CHAPTER THREE

WE all sit around a table in a café in St David's centre and the waiter takes our order.

"Eliana, are you okay? Lucy has told me everything," Beth says.

"I guess I'm still in shock," I reply, just as the waiter brings our drinks over and places them on the table.

"I know it's a lot to take in," Beth says sympathetically. "I can't believe it myself. I know Andy had girlfriends before he met your mother, but like Lucy, I don't remember a girl called Lisa ever being around."

"I've got a brother, and he's not much older than me," I say, wrapping my fingers around the mug of hot chocolate.

We remain quiet as the waiter brings our English breakfasts and places them on the table. We all dig in, eating in silence for a few moments.

"I think I want to meet Brent," I suddenly say and wait for their reaction, and they look at me intently.

"I mean, it would be nice to get to know him, but I'm so nervous and scared about it. What if he has changed his mind?"

Lucy places a warm hand on mine.

"Eliana, we will be there for you every step of the way, if you want us to be. We will even come along, but only if you are sure it's something you want to really do."

"If it's any consolation, Brent probably feels the same, sweetie," Beth says.

"He's had to deal with the news that he's had a sister out there all this time," Lucy suggests, before putting the food on her fork into her mouth.

I sit there and think about what she just said for a moment.

"Can you help me reach out to him?" I ask.

"Of course we can, Eliana," Beth replies.

We finish eating and the waiter comes over.

"Was everything okay?" he asks.

"Yes, lovely thank you," Beth replies, and he takes our empty plates away.

"So, what are you going to do for the rest of the day, Eliana?" Lucy asks.

"I think I'll go back to the house and see if I can find a number for that solicitor, Brent's mother mentioned in the letter…"

Lucy cuts me off.

"Actually, I found a letter with details for the solicitor's office. The firm has an office over by the museum. Would you like to pay them a visit?"

I nod.

"Yeah, I think we should go over before I chicken out."

Beth calls the waiter and asks for the bill. After the bill is paid, we leave and head over to the law firm.

"What was the name of the law firm you found details for?" I ask Lucy as we walk through St David's centre.

"It's called Thompson and Co."

"Eliana, don't be surprised if they tell you to make an appointment before they can see you," Beth says.

"Actually, I did make an appointment for you, Eliana," Lucy explains.

"When? How did you know I was going to want to start looking for Brent?" I ask.

"I did it before we left the house while you were getting ready. To be honest, I didn't really bank on you saying you wanted to meet your brother. I was going to go on your behalf and see what they say. The appointment is for one o'clock this afternoon," Lucy tells me.

"Lucy. You are so damn sneaky," Beth laughs.

TWENTY minutes later, we are standing outside a big, old brick building. I stare at the purple sign that says Thompson and Co Law Firm. Lucy leads the way and I follow with Beth behind. She opens the door and walks into the reception area, and we follow, where the receptionist greets us with a smile.

"Hello, welcome to Thompson and Co. Do you have an appointment?"

"Yes. It's with Mr Patrick Neilson at one, my name is Lucy Smith."

"Okay, you are a little early so let me just check if Mr Nelson is free."

The receptionist searches her computer, before pressing a few numbers into her phone.

"Hello, Mr Nelson. I have your one o'clock, Miss Smith."

She says with a smile.

"Yes sir. Thank you," she replies, before hanging up.

"If you can take a seat, Mr Nelson will be with you shortly," she tells Lucy.

We head to the plush, red seats.

"I'm so nervous, my stomach is doing somersaults," I whisper to my Aunts.

"There's absolutely nothing to worry about. It will be fine. It's just a meeting with the solicitor," Lucy reassures us just as the door opens.

A man wearing a dark navy suit appears.

"Miss Smith?"

"Hi. Yes that's me," Lucy stands up and shakes his hand.

"This is my sister Beth and my niece, whom I mentioned on the phone," she explains to him.

We take turns to shake his hand.

"If you ladies would like to follow me to my office," he suggests.

We follow him down the corridor into a big room.

"If you would like to take a seat, we can get started," Mr Nelson says, indicating to the chairs opposite his desk, that's strewn with papers and an open laptop.

"So, I understand you found a letter from a former client, Mrs Carmichael, in regards to her son Mr Brent Carmichael?" he questions.

Lucy nods and hands him the letter.

"This is the letter. As you can see Mrs Carmichael wanted her son to have a relationship with his sister, my niece. We have no idea where he is and as it states in the letter your law firm has been listed to contact for his details, should she wish to gain contact."

Mr Nelson runs his eyes over the letter.

"Hmm, I see. Mrs Carmichael was a client of my father, not mine, so I would need to open some old files up and speak to my father about this. If you leave these letters with me and your contact details I will get back to you as soon as I have some information."

We get up out of our chairs.

"Could you contact me, directly?" I ask.

"Of course," he says.

He hands me a notebook and a silver pen with his name on and

He smiles apologetically.

"Sorry I couldn't give you more information today, but this is an old client, who has previously dealt with my father who had retired. I'll be in touch soon."

He opens the door for us to leave.

"We will find Brent and when you meet your brother for the first time, we will be with you like we promised you won't be alone," Beth assures me.

Sensing my tension, Lucy changes the subject.

"Are you still working for Jose's Clothing?"

"Yeah, I'm still there. My boss Andrea is nice, she let me take the week off because of the anniversary," I tell her.

"So when are you back in work, Eliana?" Lucy asks.

"Next week."

We open the door to sunshine beaming down.

"Thank you both for coming with me today and being here for me. I love you both," I tell them.

"We love you too Eliana," Beth says. "It's a lovely day, shall we take a walk?"

I nod.

"I'd really like to go take a walk around the castle walls and take a look at the stone animals in the day."

"You'll have to count me out, I'm afraid," Lucy tells me. "I need to shoot off, I've got to go pick up Shane from his girlfriend's, but I'll give you a ring later."

"I guess it's just us then, sweetie," Beth says.

CHAPTER FOUR

IT'S been just over three weeks since we went to see

Mr Nelson and I've been trying to keep occupied to take my mind off things. At work, Andrea has me doing the floor display.

"You're so good at this kind of thing," she tells me, before she heads to the office to finish paperwork.

Suddenly a '*boo*' startles me.

"Jesus Shane. You scared the life out of me," I say punching his arm, and he laughs.

"You should see your face," he replies.

"Dumb ass. Why are you here anyway?"

"Mum told me about the letters."

"Oh, that. I'd almost forgotten," I lie.

"So, you have a brother?"

"Yeah, Brent Carmichael. That's all I know, though. I'm still waiting to hear from the solicitor," I explain.

Suddenly my phone beeps.

"Hang on a sec," I tell Shane and rush over to the counter. "It's Mr Nelson," I say trying to contain my excitement as I swipe the screen.

"Hello."

"Hello, is this Miss Eliana Stevens?"

The woman's voice on the other end is business-like and

I gulp.

"Er… yes. That's me."

"Could you come in this afternoon to see Mr Nelson?"

I tell her yes and agree to be there at four.

"I'm really sorry to have to ask this," I say to Andrea in the office and

she lifts her head up out of a file.

"Why do I have a sneaking suspicion that you need to leave early?"

I explain the situation to her and she nods.

"Of course."

She looks over at Shane browsing through t-shirts and smiles

"And yes, you can still have your lunch break."

"I really appreciate this," I tell her, before I head over to Shane.

"Let's go grab some lunch and catch up," I suggest while buttoning up my coat.

We stop at the café not far from the shop. We order bacon rolls and a can of coke.

"So cuz, how do you really feel about having a brother?" Shane asks.

"Honestly? It scares the life out of me. I mean, what if he hates me?"

Shane rolls his eyes.

"Now, why would he hate you? From what mum has said he wants to meet you. He wouldn't have written that letter otherwise.

"Hmm... "

"Besides, what's not to like? You're sweet. Kind of a freak at times but..."

I give him a kick under the table.

"I'm not a freak," I say, and

he laughs.

"Yes you are. A book freak." He pokes out his tongue. "But you're family and I love you."

"Now you're making me blush."

"You may be my cousin, but you are more like a sister. If anyone hurts you, I'll kick their ass. So Brent had better watch it."

"Aww you're so sweet," I tease.

"I'm trying to be serious here," Shane tells me, and he leans towards me. "Look, if you ever need me, all you have to do is ask."

"Aww Shane, you are going to make me cry. I love you too."

We both bite into our bacon rolls.

"I still feel nervous about meeting him though," I say between mouthfuls. "Will you come with me to the law

firm later? I don't want to bother your mother or Aunt Beth."

Shane laughs.

"Think I can fit you into my manic schedule. What time is this life changing meeting?"

"The law firm wants me to go over at four o'clock, but Andrea said I can finish at half three."

He nods.

"Right, I'll come pick you up, and we can walk over," he replies.

"Thanks, Shane."

"There was another reason I called in the shop today," he says, wiping his greasy hands along his jeans.

"There's me thinking you had my best interests at heart."

"I do," he assures me. "But I was wondering, have you heard any rumours about Alexis?"

"No, why? What's going on?"

I gasp at the image on the screen. It's Alexis, kissing some bloke and sitting on another ones lap, who has his hand inside her dress.

"Oh my God, Shane. I'm sorry, I can't believe she's done this to you."

"Yep."

I pass his phone back to him.

"What are you going to do?"

"Honestly, I don't know. Part of me wants to find these guys, kick the shit out of them and dump her, but…" he pauses.

"But what? You still love her?"

"Yeah, I do, but looking at this photo, I don't think she feels the same."

"Have you confronted her?"

He shakes his head.

"No, I haven't. I've just been avoiding her."

Suddenly, his phone starts to ring, he glances at the caller ID and swipes the screen to send it to voicemail.

"Alexis?"

"Yeah, she can wait. I'll call her when I am ready." He plunges his phone into his pocket. I get up and tuck the chair under the table.

"I'd better get back to work. I know it's only been half an hour, but the faster the day goes, the quicker I will be able to see if the solicitor has managed to track down Brent."

Shane pays the bill, and we walk back to the shop and I turn to him before I go in.

"Shane, give Alexis a ring, see what she has to say about that photo," I suggest.

He nods.

"Maybe."

"ELIANA, go grab your things. I will see you tomorrow and you can tell me what the solicitor has said," Andrea says at the end of my shift.

"Thanks. I will."

Outside the shop, Shane swings an arm over my shoulder as we walk.

"Are you ready to do this, Eli?" he asks.

"Nope. What if he's decided now he doesn't want anything to do with me after all?"

"Then he's losing out on an amazing little sister in his life," Shane replies and I smile up at him.

"I'm so glad you are with me," I reply.

CHAPTER FIVE

I open the door to the law firm. The receptionist is on the phone and there is a guy in his mid-twenties sitting there, typing into his phone. He's wearing a white polo shirt, dark blue denim jeans and white trainers. The receptionist ends the call and looks up at us with a smile.

"Hello again, Miss Stevens. Mr Nelson will be with you shortly, if you'd like to take a seat."

As we head for the seats, the guy in the seating area glances up. Shane sits next to him and I take the seat at the other side of him. After a few moments, Mr Nelson opens a door.

"Miss Stevens, if you would like to go to the room at the end of the corridor and take a seat. I will be with you in just a second.

We go into the room Mr Nelson has directed us to and I hear another door close opposite. Mr Nelson comes into the room and closes the door behind him, before taking a seat opposite us.

"How have you been, Miss Stevens?" he asks.

I laugh to take the edge off the serious atmosphere.

"Busy with work."

I introduce Shane, as Mr Nelson shuffles through papers.

"I apologise for not getting back to you sooner, but it took some digging through my father's records."

He gathers the papers, taps them into shape like a card deck and looks up with a smile.

"But to cut a long story short, we have managed to find him, and he would like to meet you today."

I gulp. This is happening so quickly.

"Today?"

Mr Nelson smiles warmly.

"Yes, today."

He takes a key out of his pocket to unlock a drawer in his desk.

"He wanted me to give you this first," he says, pulling out a crisp, white envelope.

I shake as I read the letter inside.

Dear Eliana,

I honestly didn't think that I would hear from you. I was so surprised when Mr Nelson contacted me. After all these years, I had given up thinking you would try to get in touch. I partly thought Andrew had turned you against me in some way, because I wanted nothing to do with him. That maybe he thought I shouldn't I know it's a lot to take in, finding out you have a brother. Hell, it was a shock to me too, to discover I have a little sister. I have always wanted a brother or sister. After mum had me, she didn't have any other children. When she was dying, she told me about You and Andrew. I didn't believe her at first, but then I found the DNA results. After seeing them, I decided I wanted to meet you in person. I know you probably have lots of questions, just as I have. So, if you still want to meet me, open the door in the next ten minutes, walk across the hall and open the door just opposite. If you decide not to, we can do this whenever you are ready.

Brent

I glance across to Mr Nelson, then look to Shane for some reassurance.

"He's here?" I question.

Shane turns to look at Mr Nelson.

"You mean Brent is here right now?"

"Yes. Mr Carmichael is in this building. He is eager to meet you, Miss Stevens, but as he's mentioned, he wants the final decision to be yours."

"Eli, what do you want to do? The ball is in your court." Shane asks in an urgent tone.

Glancing back at the letter in my hand, I pause to try and gather my thoughts.

"Miss Stevens, are you okay?" Mr Nelson asks.

The letter shakes in my hands.

"Would you like a glass of water, Miss Stevens?"

I look up at Mr Nelson.

"Yes. Er… no. Oh sorry, Mr Nelson. It's just that it's come as a bit of a shock."

I hold my hand out to shake Mr Nelson's hand to thank him.

"Are you going to meet him?" Shane asks.

I don't reply. Instead, I open the door of the room we are in and stare at the brown door opposite. My hands begin to tremble. Shane places his on my shoulder and squeezes it gently. I look at him for reassurance, and he nods with a smile. Reaching out, I push the handle down on the door in front of me. It goes down slowly and the door opens. I feel like I'm going to be sick. My heart races and the palms of my hands feel sweaty. The door opens wider and there he is, with his head down looking at his phone. Brent. My brother.

CHAPTER SIX

THE door handle makes noise, as I let go and Brent glances up from his phone. It's the guy who was in reception, with the white polo shirt and jeans. His eyes meet mine and we stand there in silence, just gazing at each other. Suddenly somebody clears their throat, breaking the silence. It's Shane.

"Hi. You must be Brent," he introduces himself from behind me. "I'm Shane, Eliana's cousin. I guess that makes me your cousin too."

Brent smiles and I notice he has white, even teeth.

"I guess it does."

He stands up and slowly walks towards us. Shane nudges me forward from behind and Brent stops a few meters away.

"Eliana, are you okay? You haven't said a thing," Brent asks.

I open my mouth but nothing comes out.

"You'll have to be patient with Eli, she tends to clam up when she's nervous," Shane says. He looks at me for the go ahead and I nod.

"I'm going to give you both some space and wait out in reception."

Shane says as he heads to the door.

"Give her a few minutes," he tells Brent, before leaving the room. Brent steps forward.

"I know this must be weird for you, Eliana. It's kind of strange for me too. One minute I am an only child and now I have a little sister."

I still can't find the words.

"I want you to know, I've always thought about you…"

I cut him off.

"You did? If that is true why didn't you try to contact me?" I manage to ask.

"I never worked up the courage to come and find you because for some reason, I thought Andrew wouldn't let me see you. That probably sounds like a cop out I know, but it's the truth. I just wish I had more guts to contact you before today," he explains.

I feel my eyes prickling and my hands shake even more. Brent glances down at my hands and moves forward, before reaching out and taking them into his own. Then the dam breaks. Tears fall fast and hard. He lets go of my hands before wrapping his arms around me and I break

down sobbing into his chest. The smell of Hugo Boss aftershave, fills my airways.

"Can you ever forgive me for not looking for you, sis?"

This makes me cry even harder. I wrap my arms around him, squeezing him harder, and he responds by squeezing back. We stay like this for a few minutes, until I get my sobbing under control.

"Brent, you are the only part of dad, I have left. Just looking at you, is like seeing the old photos of him when he was younger. There is nothing to forgive," I say finally.

"Thank you, Eliana. Maybe we should get out of here. Perhaps go somewhere to talk some more?"

"We could go back to the house, or maybe the castle gardens. It gets full sun this time of day."

"The castle gardens sound perfect. I don't know about you, but I could use some fresh air," Brent says.

He steps back a little, before reaching up to wipe the tears from under my eyes and I smile at him.

"I can't believe you are my brother. I've always wanted a brother or sister."

Suddenly there is a knock on the door and Mr Nelson's head appears around the door.

"Is everything okay in here?" he asks.

"Yes. We are actually just about to leave," Brent says.

"Thank you for everything you have done," I say.

Brent extends his hand.

"Mr Nelson, I can't thank you enough for putting me in touch with Eliana."

Mr Nelson shakes Brent's hand.

"I finally have the sister I've always wanted, and I am never letting her go."

Mr Nelson looks pleased.

"I'm glad that I could help you find each other. It makes my job worthwhile, when there is a happy ending."

We follow Mr Nelson out of the room to the reception area, where Shane is waiting. When he sees us he stands up.

"Is everything okay, Eli?"

I walk over to him and hug him.

"Thank you for coming with me. I think everything is going to be okay now. I have a big brother," I whisper.

He gives me a tight squeeze.

"I'm so happy for you," he whispers back.

Shane steps back and looks over at Brent.

"My mother and Aunt Beth can't wait to meet you, but you've probably had enough excitement for one day."

Brent exhales.

"Yeah, it's a lot to take in, Eliana and myself still have lots to talk about. Maybe next time."

"We're going to walk over to the castle gardens. Do you want to come along, or do you have plans?" I ask Shane.

"If you are okay, I'm going to shoot off and talk to Alexis," Shane replies.

"I'm alright," I assure him. "I'll call you later."

I hug him.

"You should go confront Alexis, she's got a lot of explaining to do," I tell him.

"Yeah, she does. If you need me, just call and I'll have mam drop me off."

He turns to Brent.

"It was nice to meet you, Brent. Don't hurt Eli, she's been hurt too much already."

CHAPTER SEVEN

WE sit on the bench in the gardens at the side of the castle.

"I'm glad we finally met, Eliana," Brent says, and he takes out a small, white envelope from his pocket.

"I have something to show you."

He offers me an envelope.

"What's this?" I ask, taking it.

"Open it."

I open it and there is a letter with a photograph of a child.

"It's me."

I recognise the scrawly handwriting in the letter. It's my father's.

Brent,

I only just found out about you from your mother. If she had told me sooner, I would have been there for you. I hope it's not too late to be a part of your life now. Your mum was my first love. I loved her so much, but I worked away a lot and the more I was away.

That was when I met Natasha. She came from an abusive relationship. It all happened between us while I was helping her escape. I helped her to heal. We fell in love. I know how that sounds, but we found each other when we needed it the most. I couldn't help my feelings. I took the coward's way out and walked away from your mother with no explanation. I don't know how she found me after all these years, but I'm glad she did. I know you probably think very little of me. I have a daughter now, so you have a little sister. Her name is Eliana. She's smart, bubbly and has a loving nature. She's exactly like her mum. You would love her, even if you don't want me to be part of your life, I hope that if you ever get a chance you will be part of hers.

There is a photo of her attached to this letter. If I die before we have a chance to meet, please look after my little Eli bear. She doesn't deserve the hate or the pain I have caused.

Andrew

"Wow," I say handing the letter back to Brent.

"Yeah, I know. As much as I hate him for what he did to my mum, I am glad he told me about you," he replies.

"Brent, would you have come looking for me, if I hadn't spoken to the law firm?" I ask.

He grabs my hand and turns to face me.

"Eli, the moment I found out I had a sister, I had a million questions, but I didn't want to ask mum. I didn't want to hurt her by talking about you, the child her first love went on to have. I know how bad that sounds and…"

I cut him off.

"Brent, I get it. It would have been hard on her."

He pulls me in for a hug.

"Eli, I wish things were different, and we grew up together, but we can't change the past. All we can do now is look to the future and I want to spend the time that we lost, getting to know you. The moment you opened that door back at Mr Nelson's law firm, I was lost for words. I wanted to tell you then who I was but thought that you would run and your boyfriend would kick my ass," he explains.

I laugh.

"You thought Shane was my boyfriend?"

"Yeah, the way he was with you. His arm on your back and standing so close to you. He was so protective."

I sit up and stare at him. Suddenly, I can't help it, a massive smile fills my face.

"Shane will find it so funny when I tell him, you thought he was my boyfriend."

Brent laughs.

"I'll bet."

"Brent, ever since my parents died, he's taken on the big brother role. He's my cousin and also my best friend. We are really close. My Aunts are the same, always fussing and being protective."

"So do you have a boyfriend or a girlfriend?" Brent asks.

"Nope. I haven't really had the head for a love life, but I do like boys in case you were wondering."

We laugh.

"You should come to the house on Sunday for lunch. You can meet everyone then," I suggest.

He stands up.

"I'm not sure I am ready to meet everyone else just yet," he says pacing back and forth.

"Brent, you've already met Shane. There's only Aunt Beth and Lucy left. My grandparents on both sides, died long before I was born."

I wait for a moment, but he doesn't respond.

"I know they are both excited to meet you. It was actually Lucy that set up the meeting with Mr Nelson because she knew I'd be too nervous, but I am so glad she did."

He stops pacing and looks at me.

"Okay, I'll come for dinner," he says.

He comes back over to the bench, and we spend the next hour talking, before he says he has to leave.

"Shall I call you a taxi?" he asks.

"No, I'm fine. I think I'll just sit here for a while longer," I say and watch as he heads towards the gate of the gardens.

CHAPTER EIGHT

I'M still on the bench in the gardens when daylight turns to darkness. I listen to sounds of the city go by in the distance. I close my eyes.

It has been a long day, with meeting Brent. I'm not sure I've wrapped my head around the fact I have a brother. I feel all jittery and know that there is no way I will sleep, so I decide to move over to the grass. I lie down, place my bag behind my head and gaze up at the stars. I can see Orion's Belt, three stars close together in a row. Star gazing is something I love. I used to do it with mum out in the garden. I feel like she's near when I block everything else out to look at the stars. I like to believe she is one of them. The brightest star in the sky.

"You."

A voice shouts from the shadows. I jump.

"Jesus. Will you quit doing that?"

I look around, but I see nothing.

"Hello?"

Nothing.

"Coward. Hiding in the shadows, trying to scare people," my voice sails into the darkness.

The bushes rustle as a twig snaps. I glance around the gardens, there's still nobody in sight. Another twig snaps behind me and I spin around quickly and stand up.

"Listen wise guy, if you are going to attack me then you are in for a surprise."

Nothing.

"I took self-defence classes and I will kick your ass."

I sound more courageous than I feel.

"I want you out of my gardens," the voice whispers urgently.

I stand frozen to the spot.

"Leave now," the voice booms.

"Stop ordering me about."

I hope my voice doesn't sound too shaky.

"Go back to wherever you came from. These gardens are open to the public and don't belong exclusively to you."

I pause when two bright, green eyes appear in the bush in front of me.

"I am not going anywhere. Do you really think two specs of green light, that look like eyes, will scare me?"

The bushes rustle.

"You can try all the tricks you want to get me to leave, but I'm not going anywhere," I say not taking my eyes off the green in the bushes.

I turn around and bend down to grab my phone. Suddenly, I'm pushed forward onto my stomach and something heavy is on my back holding me down.

"I warned you. When I told you to stay away, you should have listened the first time."

"Who are you?"

"You've picked the wrong garden to keep coming back to," the voice whispers in my ear, giving me goosebumps. "I've been watching you all day with your boyfriend. I knew you were trouble the minute you came into my gardens. You should have left when he did. Now, this is your final warning, next time you won't be so lucky."

In a flash, the weight on my back is gone. I quickly scramble to gather my bag and phone. Gasping for breath, I run and jump back over the gate of the gardens. I glance over the gate into the darkness but I don't see anybody. I walk a little down the road, before I see a taxi and flag it down to go home. Panting, I climb in and give the driver my address.

When the taxi pulls up outside my address, I pay the driver before climbing out. I'm still shaking as I take out my keys to unlock the door. I dive into the house, slam the front door and put the catch on. My heart is racing. I close my eyes for a moment to try and steady my nerves. I felt helpless, pinned on the floor by somebody I couldn't see.

What on earth was I thinking retaliating like that?

I rush into the kitchen, get out a bottle of vodka, pour myself a small glass, then knock it back, before I pour myself another. It burns as it goes down, but it calms me a little. Placing the vodka back in the fridge and the empty glass in the sink, I walk back into the living room and collapse on the sofa.

CHAPTER NINE

"You have been warned. I gave you a chance and you decided to ignore it. Now you will pay."

The voice says from the darkness, and arms take me from behind.

"I told you there would be consequences," the voice says as one hand moves from my body to push my head to the side. Pain shoots through me as my neck is attacked.

I jump up in bed, sweat pouring off me. My phone rings from the bedside cabinet and I reach over and pick it up. I swipe across the screen and answer.

"Hey, Shane. What are you doing up so early?"

I find his laughter on the other end comforting.

"Eli, it's nearly nine. I wanted to check in with you after yesterday. How did it go with Brent after I left?" he asks.

"It was good. Kind of awkward at first, but once we got talking, it was like he has always been in my life. He actually showed me a letter dad wrote to him, along with a photo of me."

"Really?"

"Yeah. I think in dad's own way it was as if he knew he did wrong by Brent and his mother, but his last words to Brent were that he wanted him to be a part of my life."

"So, when are you going to see him again?"

"Actually, I've invited him to Sunday dinner. I know Aunt Beth and Lucy can't wait to meet him, so I thought we could all have some dinner together."

"Sounds like a plan. We…"

I cut him off.

"Oh, you never guess what he thought when we came into the office?"

"What's that then?"

"He thought you were my boyfriend."

"Bloody hell. What gave him that idea?"

"He said because of the way you were so protective of me and how close we were." I laugh.

"Sounds reasonable."

"He also asked if I had a boyfriend."

Shane bursts into laughter.

"He's only met you yesterday, and he's already doing the big brother thing. I like him already. It's going to be fun when you bring a guy home to meet the family. No man will want to hurt you, when we are around."

"Very funny, not. I'm never letting you meet any guy I start dating."

"Yeah, right. You just keep telling yourself that. I'd better shoot off. Mum wants me to go to the shops with her. See you Sunday."

I wish him well with shopping with Lucy and hang up the phone. It's going to be a long day at work, as I agreed to cover and work the late shift.

My shift is winding down. I am tidying the rails, when Shane's girlfriend walks in with a group of girls. I can't be bothered to make small talk with the little cheat, so I go back behind the till to empty boxes, hoping she'll pass quickly.

"So, Alexis, what are you going to do about Shane? Kick him to the curb? I know there are lots of girls are waiting for him to be available."

I hear the smirk in the tone.

"Why would I dump Shane?"

I hear Alexis talking and can tell she's chewing gum.

"So what was the other night about then? That other guy you kissed?"

Now, they've got my attention. I crouch even further behind the till.

"There were two guys, actually," another girl's voice pipes up.

They laugh and I have to stop myself from rising off the floor and jumping over the till.

"Big deal. I am the best thing to happen to Shane," Alexis says, "If I want to kiss random guys, then I will. It's not like I fuck other ones behind his back."

"Not yet but you came pretty close to screwing his best friend's brother Jake, the other night," Miss Smirk says.

I hear them all giggle.

"True but I don't do drunk sex with any guys," Alexis sighs.

I've heard enough. My knees creak as I rise to the counter and

Alexis's face drops when she sees me.

"Shane didn't mention that I work here, then?" I say glaring at she glances between me and her friends.

"I did hear everything that was said just now."

I enjoy watching her squirm.

"I'd go tell my cousin what you've been doing behind his back, if I were you."

Alexis opens her mouth to speak but nothing comes out.

LM EVANS

"Shane doesn't need somebody like you in his life," I tell her before she storms out of the shop. I grab my phone from the shelf above the till.

Hey Shane, the photos you saw the other day with Alexis on some guys lap, well I just heard a thing or two about them. She was just in here bragging to her friends.

I hit send and wait for the call.

"Are you serious, Eli? She was in the shop? Bragging?"

"Sorry to be the bearer of bad news, but yeah. I did order her to tell you. From what I can make out, she has only kissed other guys."

"Yeah? Well kissing other guys is a step too far for me. I have to go. Thanks for the info."

"Glad to hear you won't put up with that shit," I tell him. "I've always got your back, Shane. You know that."

I go get my bag from the back room as it's time to close up and set the alarms.

"How did it go yesterday with your new brother?" Andrea asks as she locks the shutter.

"He's lovely. So sweet and caring."

Andrea laughs.

"So there was no need for all that panic, then?"

"He was just as nervous as I was."

"I'm so glad it went well."

Andrea puts the keys into her bag.

"So, tell me. What does he look like? This mysterious brother of yours," she asks, as

- 48 -

"Mid-twenties, dark hair, tall, athletic…"

"Like him over there?" Andrea nods in the direction behind me. "He's been watching us since we came out."

I turn around and see him. Brent, leaning against the wall between two shops. I wave and he waves back.

Andrea laughs.

"I was beginning to think he was planning to rob us."

Brent walks over and he doesn't hold back, he takes me by surprise and wraps his arms around me tightly, before letting go and taking a step back. I feel the heat in my cheeks.

"Brent, this is my boss, Andrea. Andrea, this is Brent. My brother."

Brent shakes Andreas's hand.

"Nice to meet you, Brent," Andrea says. She turns to me. "Thanks for today Eli. I'll see you Monday."

We stand there and watch Andrea leave.

"So, how long have you been here?" I ask.

"Not that long. I wanted to see the place you work. I was going to come in but you were busy with some girls earlier. So I decided to go for a walk, then come wait for you when you finished," he explains.

"Oh, you were here when Alexis and her fan club came by then? You should have just come in…"

Suddenly I am cut off as I'm pushed from behind and Brent catches me.

"You okay?" he asks.

"Yeah," I say and I turn around to see Alexis scowling.

"You bitch. You couldn't resist, could you? You ran and told Shane before I even had a chance to tell him."

Alexis lunges at me but Brent pushes in.

"I don't think so, sweetheart."

He positions his arms between hers to block the attack, and she stands back. She glares at me standing behind Brent.

"Are you freaking kidding me right now? You cause shit and hide behind your boyfriend."

"Brother." Brent informs Alexis, as she stands there laughing.

"As her brother, I'm telling you this; lay one more finger on my sister and I will have you done for assault."

I step out at the side of Brent in time to see her shocked face, before she storms off, and he turns to face me.

"So, I'm guessing there is a story there?"

"Isn't there just."

"Why not fill me in over dinner?"

"If you're sure?"

"I'll cook," Brent says.

"That really would be nice," I say as we walk arm in arm to the bus station.

CHAPTER TEN

FORTY minutes later, we step off the bus on the outskirts of the city. After a ten-minute walk, we stop outside a house. Brent walks past the front door to the side of it to another door. He pulls out a set of keys and unlocks the door. I notice a set of stairs with a doorway at the top. He glances back at me.

"It's a first floor flat," he says as he steps back. "After you."

I walk in and he follows me, closing the door behind him. He guides me to a living room with dark wood flooring, a black corner sofa and grey cushions. I notice the walls are painted grey and cream. Brent steps around me and walks further into the room and puts his keys and phone on the fireplace.

"Welcome to my humble abode. I'll go stick some food on for us. Is there anything in particular that you don't like?"

I shrug.

"I'm not really a fish fan, but otherwise I am good," I reply, my eyes taking in the surroundings.

"Okay, good. Why don't you grab a seat? I'll be back in a moment."

He walks out of the room and I place my bag on the sofa and sit down. Glancing around, I notice a big television on the wall above the cream fireplace, with an electric fire. There is a photo of a woman holding a baby in a silver frame on one end, on the other, there is a photo of the woman alone. I stand up and walk closer to take a better look. Her long brown hair is just above her shoulders, against a pink cardigan. Her eyes are big and brown, and she's smiling.

"That's my mother," Brent says, making me jump.

"She was beautiful. You have her nose, but you have dad's eyes and mouth," I tell him.

"She really was beautiful. My world. I miss her so much," he says wistfully. "But I know she's in a better place now."

I nod, as I don't

Suddenly Brent changes the subject.

"I have a sausage pasta bake I made in the oven for us. Is that okay?"

"Sounds great. I'm sorry if it upsets you when I bring dad up," I say, not wanting to hurt his feelings.

"It's fine. He was your dad too. I've made peace with the fact I look like him. The way I see it, if it wasn't for him I wouldn't have you." he replies as the door to downstairs opens.

"Brent. What are you cooking?" a voice rushes up.

Blue eyes land on me.

"Well hello, sweetness."

"Back off, Owen. This is Eliana, my sister," Brent explains as Owen stands right in front of me.

"Your sister?"

"Yep."

"Do you have a boyfriend, Eliana?" Owen asks, putting emphasis on my name. He gets a shove from Brent.

"Out of bounds, mate," Brent tells him.

I laugh.

"I'm flattered, Owen, but you aren't my type."

"Eliana, you crush me," he says holding his chest like he's in pain.

"Are you staying, or are you off to Joanne's?" Brent asks.

"Yeah, I'm off over to Joanne's tonight. Just came by to grab a few things."

"Eliana, this idiot is my flatmate," Brent explains. "I swear he's not normally a flirt, even though he's got a girlfriend."

"Nice to meet you, Eliana. I was just kidding about. My boy Brent doesn't normally bring girls back here to talk…"

Brent cuts him off.

"Dude, really?"

Owen bursts into laughter, and he takes my hand and kisses it.

"Well, it's been nice meeting you, young lady. Maybe next time we will have more time to talk, but I do need to shoot, my girl is waiting for me."

Owen goes into what I assume is his bedroom and comes back out with a bag.

"See you soon."

"So, does anybody else live here or is it just you two?" I ask as we hear the door close.

"Just me and Owen. We've been friends since high school. He's harmless and a good guy really, even if he is a bit full on."

I smile at him.

"He's cool."

"Are you working tomorrow?"

I shake my head.

"Nope. I'm off until Monday."

"I was wondering if…"

Suddenly the buzzer goes off in the kitchen and a lovely smell wafts through.

"The pasta bake."

He gets up to go into the kitchen and I follow. The kitchen is small. It has a male presence with black units and white appliances. Brent goes over to the oven and opens it.

"It smells delicious," I say.

My mouth waters, as he takes the dish out of the oven and moves a spoon around the edges of the dish, before placing it back in the oven.

"I hope you are hungry. It will be ready in about ten minutes."

"What were you going to say before the buzzer went off," I ask.

"Don't worry. It doesn't matter," he replies, as he holds the kitchen door open.

"Let me give you the guided tour."

"Well, this is the kitchen," he laughs and I smile at him.

"I think I can see that," I reply with playful sarcasm.

He laughs, walks out of the room and stops in front of another door.

"The bathroom."

He points to the door Owen came out of earlier.

"Owen's room?"

"Clever girl." He nods, and then opens another door.

"My room."

There are navy walls inside. A king-size bed stands in the middle of the room and there is a TV on the wall. The duvet and curtains, in navy, match.

"I wasn't expecting you to be living in a flat," I say. "I thought perhaps you would be still living at your mother's house."

He sits on the bed and kicks off his shoes.

"I wish that was possible, but after mum died I couldn't afford to live there on my own. So I had to give it up and move in with Owen for a while. Then, when my trust fund came through from my grandparents, when I turned twenty-one, I bought this place and Owen moved in. The rest is history as they say."

The buzzer on the cooker goes off again.

"Jeez, that was quick," he says, as he gets off the bed and walks past me into the kitchen. I follow, and he takes the food out the oven and turns it off, before plating the pasta bake.

"Here you go. I hope you enjoy it," he says passing me a plate and fork, before picking up his own.

We take our food into the living room and sit on the sofa. He turns the TV on and there is a film on Film 4. I dig my fork into the pasta.

"Thanks for this. It looks delicious."

"You're welcome, it's not every day I find out I have a sister and have a chance to cook for her." He smirks, before he digs into his own pasta.

It's not really my kind of film but I'm happy just to relax with him. Every so often, I find myself glancing at him not really believing this is happening.

When the film finishes its most eleven.

"Is that really the time?" I say rising off the sofa.

"Eliana, I know it's late and you are not working tomorrow, so would you prefer to stay the night instead of going home?"

"I…"

"I have some clothes you can borrow to wear to sleep in."

"What about Owen? Would he mind me crashing out on the sofa?"

Brent reaches out and catches my hand.

"Eliana, you are my little sister. I'm sure he wouldn't mind. Besides, you will have my bed and I will crash in Owen's room as he's staying at his girlfriend's house tonight."

"Okay, I would like that, thanks," I reply. I don't relish the idea of going out into the cold.

"Awesome! I'll go grab some shorts and a T-shirt for you to change, then we can watch Rambo."

I roll my eyes.

"Rambo? Really?"

He goes into the bedroom and a few minutes later he walks back in wearing blue shorts and a black sports tank top.

"Your clothes are at the end of the bed."

I go into the bedroom to change. The white T-shirt is more like a nightshirt, as it falls just to just above my knees. The shorts are just about showing. I walk out of the bedroom into the living room.

"Come on, sis," Brent says tapping the seat beside him and I smile.

"Brent, you are an amazing guy. I am so glad you are my brother. Do you have a girlfriend?" I ask.

He shakes his head.

"Not exactly. There's a girl I like, but she's with another guy," he pauses. "He's a tool towards her, treats her like shit, yet, she can't see how bad he treats her. So we are just friends."

"I'm sure this girl, whoever she is, will see the light soon," I reply.

"Maybe, but until then, I am happy to be single," he says, and we sit on the sofa as Rambo lights up the TV.

CHAPTER ELEVEN

THE noise of a door shutting startles me. I open my eyes and glance around the room forgetting where I am for a moment. Then I remember, I'm in Brent's room. I swing my feet over the edge of the bed and throw the covers back as I ease myself out of the bed. I walk over to the door and open it to find myself facing Owen and Brent talking quietly.

"Morning," I say.

They both turn to look at me.

"Guess that answers my question," Owen says. "I was just asking Brent why he's in my room. Nice to see you again, Eliana." Owen gets up off the chair and comes over to give me a kiss on the cheek.

"Brent, can I use the bathroom please?" I ask.

"You don't have to ask. Go ahead. Do you remember where it is?" he laughs.

I step around Owen awkwardly.

"Yeah, thanks."

"Nice set of legs," I hear Owen say as the bathroom door closes.

Once I am done in the bathroom, I head back into Brent's room to change out of the shorts and T-shirt and back into my work uniform. I grab my things and walk out of the room into the living room to see a shirtless Owen, lounging on the one side of the corner sofa.

"Hey, darling. Do you wanna pick your jaw up off the floor, or do you want to keep ogling my gorgeous body?" he says smirking.

I feel my colour rise.

"I wasn't."

I can't say any more; it feels like I've been caught with my hand in the cookie jar.

Brent senses the awkwardness.

"Hey dick, go put a shirt on," he orders.

"Nah, I'm good. I quite like seeing your sister squirm at the sight of my hotness," Owen replies.

"I think I need to go home now," I say.

"You haven't had breakfast," Brent says.

"I'll be fine," I assure him. "I'm going to grab a sausage and egg bagel on the way home. I'm going to do my hair, then I'll make a move."

"Okay," Brent says. "Just give me five, I'll get dressed and come with you." With that he dashes to the bedroom.

I take my brush and bobble out of my bag and head to the mirror. I make a start on my hair, brushing it and pulling it back to put the bobble in. Suddenly, I feel a hot breath on my neck.

"I know you liked looking at my body," Owen whispers in my ear. He kisses my neck, I jump and my heart starts to race.

"You have a girlfriend, you shouldn't be touching or flirting with other girls," I whisper back as I step away from him.

"Maybe, but I do like the thrill of the chase," he says moving in, "There is nothing better than fresh meat."

He steps back and walks around me to go into his room and closes the door behind him. I'm completely stunned. Suddenly Brent returns.

"Everything okay?" he asks.

"Yeah, sure. I'm okay. Thanks for letting me stay last night," I smile.

"Come on, let's go grab a bus into town to go feed you."

"You do know I'm not a baby, right? I'm twenty years old," I laugh.

He looks thoughtful.

"You know what? I just realised I don't know your birthday."

"It's the fifth of March. How about yours?"

"It's next week, actually, but I don't really celebrate. Not since mum died."

He sprays on some aftershave, and I put my hands on my hips.

"That doesn't answer my question, What date is it?"

"It's the second of March, but as I said, it's just another day. Nothing worth celebrating."

He opens the door to the stairs and I follow him out.

"Brent, do you believe in the supernatural?"

He glances back at me.

"That's a pretty random question."

"Well?"

He turns back towards the stairs and I follow him down.

"Not really, I suppose. I don't walk under ladders or open an umbrella indoors, or anything like that, but as in ghosts and stuff like that, I don't really believe. Why?"

"Just being curious and trying to find out more about you."

We step outside.

"Are you working today?" I ask.

"Yeah, I am later. On the night shift. Do you have any plans today?"

"Not really. I'm just going to veg out in front of the TV and have a lazy Saturday."

"Some people get all the luck," he laughs, and we head towards the bus stop.

CHAPTER TWELVE

AFTER I leave Brent, I catch the bus home and jump into the shower, before I collapse on the sofa. I think about what he said about the supernatural. It reminded me of my dream, and the incident the other night in the gardens, on the side of the castle. I can't shake off the eeriness of it. Whoever it was that pushed me down, was just doing it to scare people. It was probably a drunk or some arse like Owen. The green eyes were probably a trick of the light.

There is no such thing as vampires and werewolves. Only in books. I love going to the castle gardens in the evening, as it's usually so relaxing. I can see the stars more clearly when I lie on the grass. I'm going back tonight and if that twerp shows up again threatening me, I won't be running away again.

I must have dozed off thinking about what had happened,

and I awake to darkness and my phone vibrating on the floor. Stretching over, I pick up the phone and swipe across the screen. It's Shane.

"Hi."

"Hey cuz. Did I wake you?"

I yawn.

"Yeah, it's fine though. I needed to get up. I passed out on the sofa watching TV when I came home earlier. What's up?"

"Where did you go last night?"

"I stayed at Brent's. He surprised me, met me at work as we were closing and asked if I wanted to go back to his place for some food. We ate and watched a film."

"You stayed?"

"It got late, so I stayed in his room, and he stayed in his friends room. His flatmate is a bit of a flirt though," I say, rolling my eyes.

"Sounds like you have an admirer," he laughs.

"Don't even go there. Owen has a girlfriend, and he was really trying it on. Dick. Brent told him to back off as well but the minute Brent was out the room, he upped his moves."

"A player then?"

"I swear I don't like him. He can flirt all he wants, it won't work."

Shane laughs again.

"My tough little cuz."

"Shane, it's not funny. He's one slimeball."

"Eliana, chill. Jesus, you don't have to shout. I'm only messing. I bet Brent would kick his ass if he found out he tried it on with you. As amusing as your story is about the slimeball is, the reason I called is because Alexis was pissed off when I went to speak to her yesterday. I thought I should warn you in case she turns up at your work causing drama."

I remember yesterday.

"Actually, you are a little late off the mark there. She turned up after my boss left. She gave me one push from behind. Luckily, Brent caught me or I would have face planted the floor."

"I am so sorry, Eli. That's me and her, done. She doesn't get to touch you and get away with it."

"Shane, don't end things with her because of me."

"Eliana, it's not just that. There're those guys, remember?"

"Well, you can make up for your bad choices tomorrow and wash up after dinner. Remember, you, Aunt Lucy and Beth are coming over to meet Brent."

"Oh yeah. Mum is buzzing with excitement. She's with Aunt Beth now, along with a few bottles of wine. That boy won't know what's hit him when he meets the family tomorrow."

"They will both be hungover tomorrow," I say giggling. "That should be fun. I'm going to have to say goodnight now. I need to go to the shop before it shuts."

"Okay, cuz. See you tomorrow."

I plug my phone in to charge, before rushing upstairs to change into some fresh clothes. I take a blanket from the drawer, before coming back downstairs. Then grab the backpack from under the stairs to put the blanket inside, along with my purse. I shove on a hoodie and throw my bag over my shoulders, before grabbing my phone from the charger and my keys on the side table, and head out.

CHAPTER THIRTEEN

AFTER a call to the shop to grab some tins of carrots and some gravy for Sunday lunch, I catch a bus into town and walk towards the castle gardens. At the side of the castle, I pause for a moment to take my phone out of my pocket. I switch on the torch and shine it over the darkness of the gardens. Nothing but blackness greets me. Suddenly footsteps break the silence.

"You lost something, little lady?"

I turn to face a man and I barely make out his face in the dark, but he looks old.

"Er... no. I thought I heard someone," I lie.

"A young lady like you shouldn't be out on her own after dark in a place like this," the old man says before shuffling off.

When he's out of sight I put my phone back inside my hoodie pocket. I make my way to the gates and climb over. As my feet hit the ground, I take my phone out and put the torch back on. Again, I shine it around the gardens. Nothing. I am the only person here. Instead of settling on the grass near the bush like I've done on previous nights. I take my bag off my back, pull out the blanket and lay it on the grass near the path in the middle of the gardens. Before dropping my bag onto the blanket, I scrunch it up into a ball to use as a pillow, and lie down on the blanket. I switch off the torch and place it beside me. I lie there in silence for nearly three hours, completely alone, listening to the traffic on the high street until it becomes less busy. It is a lot quieter now than when I first came into the gardens. Picking up my phone I check the time. It's almost midnight.

"You again," the voice startles me, I drop my phone and sit up and glance around.

"I am not scared of you," I say before I am pushed backwards.

My eyes close and it takes me a few moments to realise what has happened. I feel a pressure on my chest and open my eyes to see something above me. I freeze at the sight of the looming animal, before my senses kick in and I try to push it off. It takes a few moments before I manage to get it off me and sit up.

"Okay jackass. This is some cheap shot. Trying to scare me with this… your pet?"

The big, catlike animal paces in circles as it glares at me.

"I'm not afraid of big cats, so your plan isn't working if you are trying to scare me again," I say with feigned confidence.

There is no retaliation.

"What are you? Some guy that gets off on scaring women?" I shout into the darkness.

I stand up and walk slowly towards the catlike creature. It stops pacing as I approach it, so I gently crouch down and hold my hand out to the animal.

"Hey there, big guy," I say, trying to not scare it.

Its eyes are luminous, glowing bright green. My heart is racing and I try to swallow the lump stuck in my throat. The cat's head moves into the hand I'm holding out. I bring my other hand up and use both my hands to stroke its head.

"Hey cat, you're not so scary are you?" I rub the cat's fur as I look around the gardens, looking for the owner.

"Now, if your master wasn't such a bossy ass and showed himself…" I pause as the cat pulls away.

"Hey big guy, where are you going?" I ask the cat.

I step back as it bares its teeth. We stare at each other before it turns around and disappears into the darkness. I bend down to pick up my phone and turn the flash on.

"Here, puss."

The light picks up nothing. The cat has disappeared. I don't relish the thought of hearing that voice tell me to leave again, so I decide to head home. I put the phone back into my hoodie pocket, snatch the blanket off the ground, before shoving it into my bag. I take another look into the blackness, sling my bag over my shoulder and head for home.

Chapter Fourteen

I'M peeling potatoes for Sunday lunch, when there is a tap at the door. It's Aunt Lucy and Shane.

"Hey sweetie, something smells good," Lucy says, making her way through to the kitchen.

"Must be the lamb in the oven."

Shane follows suit.

"I am freaking starving."

Lucy rolls her eyes.

"Well, Eliana is an awesome cook," Shane says.

"She learned from the best, her father," Beth says as she walks in.

Suddenly I feel hemmed in.

"Why don't you all go take a seat in the living room?" I suggest. "I'm just peeling the potatoes. It won't take long."

They head into the living room.

"Can I get you a drink before I finish the potatoes?" I shout to them.

"Eliana, you carry on what you are doing and Shane can make us both a cup of tea," Lucy calls back.

Shane comes back into the kitchen to make tea and I finish the potatoes, set the table, before following him back into the living room. Beth, curious as ever, turns to Shane.

"So, what is this Brent like?"

Shane places the tea on the coffee table.

"Pretty cool. He seems quiet and from what Eli has said, he sounds protective already."

Shane goes on to explain about Brent mistaking him for my boyfriend and my Aunts laugh.

"Well, that doesn't surprise me at all. You two are pretty close," Beth says.

Suddenly the ringing of my phone interrupts us and I swipe across the screen.

"It's Brent," I whisper.

My Aunts sit up, perched like birds.

"Hey, Eliana."

"Hey Brent."

Everyone's eyes are on me.

"I'm outside. Not sure which is the right house, though."

"Just a sec, I'll come to the front door."

I walk towards the front door and open it. I step on to the path and look up the street and notice he's five doors up.

"Over here," I say waving.

He waves back, walks towards the house and up the path and hang up the phone.

"I think I got a little lost," he says as he stops on the garden path, in front of me.

"No worries. I'm just glad you're here."

He smiles and gives me a hug.

"Ready to meet the rest of the family?"

"I'm a little nervous but yeah, I am."

It's then that Shane appears.

"Are we eating on the garden path, or are you two planning on coming inside with the rest of us?"

"My apologies for Shane," I say leading the way through the house, "But he likes to think he's a comedian."

I poke my tongue out playfully at him.

"I need to check on the lamb."

I give Shane a playful punch in the belly as I pass and he moves out the way to let Brent through.

"Hey man. Good to see you again," he says.

"You too. I'm glad you were with Eliana the other day with all that business with Alexis. Did you manage to get to the bottom of it?" Brent asks.

"Yeah I dumped her. After what she did to Eliana, especially outside of her work, it was a no-go…"

Lucy cuts him off.

"What did Alexis do to Eliana?"

Shane swears under his breath.

"She pushed Eliana."

Beth gasps.

"The little madam."

"Eli might have been hurt if Brent wasn't there to catch her," Shane explains.

"Eliana, did you get hurt?" Lucy calls.

I enter the room and shake my head.

"No. It's all fine now."

"That girl. Wait until I see her. She will get a piece of my mind! Nobody lays a hand on my family." Lucy warns.

"Chill, mum. Meet Brent." Shane comes to the rescue.

Brent steps forward.

"Hi, Mrs Smith."

Lucy gets up off the chair.

"Brent, we'll have none of that, you can call me Aunt Lucy or Lucy." She says as she reaches over to him and pulls him into a hug.

"I can't believe how much you look like Andy when he was younger."

"Lucy. Leave the poor boy alone." Beth rushes over.

"Brent, I am your Aunt Beth."

Lucy steps back and Beth steps forward to give him a quick hug.

"And you," Lucy says looking at Shane, "You need to pick better girlfriends, not crazy nuts."

"I've said sorry," Shane says. "I can't help it if girls fall for me and end up complete psychos," he says under his breath, as Lucy clips the back of his head.

"You were taught to treat women better, Shane."

"Man, the women in this family have ears like bats," Shane says, earning another clip.

"Let's get this dinner done," I say.

Shane mouths a thank you, as my Aunts descend on Brent with years' worth of questions.

"So Brent, do you have a girlfriend?" Lucy asks as we are eating and he gulps down his lunch.

"Erm… no. I don't. I've been on a few dates but nothing serious."

Beth narrows her eyes.

"I'm usually too busy with work for girls," he adds quickly.

"I hear you have a birthday coming up," Lucy says and he nods.

"How old will you be?" Beth asks.

"Twenty-six in a few days' time."

"When were you born?" Shane asks.

"March second, ninety-four."

"Why, Eliana is the fifth March," Lucy says excitedly.

"We should do something to celebrate," Beth suggests.

Brent puts his knife and fork on an empty plate.

"I don't really celebrate my birthday since mum died."

"Really?" both my Aunts chorus.

"I'll probably be working all week, as there is some big concert at the Principality Stadium. The band will be staying at the hotel," Brent explains.

"That's such a shame," Beth says, looking disappointed.

"What do you have planned, Eliana for your birthday?" Lucy asks.

"I was thinking of just staying in and ordering food from that new Indian place in town," I reply.

"That that sounds nice, but…"

"Hey mum," Shane interrupts, "I was thinking of going to see what's on at the cinema this week. Do you want to go?"

I love my cousin for trying to distract my Aunt. I glance at Beth, and she gives me a knowing smile.

"I wanted to try that fish thing where you put your feet in a tank, and they eat the dead skin," I remark.

"Ugh." Shane says.

I turn to Lucy.

"I don't want to try it on my own. Would you and Aunt Beth come along on my birthday?"

"Oh that sounds like fun." Lucy replies sounding unconvinced. I mentioned to Beth about a pamper day.

"Maybe we girls could do that in the daytime for your birthday?"

"Yeah, that sounds like a plan," I reply.

"Yuck. Why would you put your stinky feet in a tank for them poor fish..." Shane is cut off by Lucy.

"Hey, my feet don't stink, you cheeky sod."

Brent laughs.

"We have a pamper suite in our hotel. It comes as a package. I can book you all in for two hours as my birthday present to Eliana."

"Brent, you can't do that. It's way too much money." I protest.

"I won't take no for an answer," Brent says. "It's the first time I can actually do something for you on your birthday and I want to make up for the birthdays I've missed."

I push my chair back a little and reach over to hug him.

"Thank you so much. You don't have to make anything up to me," I say as he squeezes me with one arm.

"Brent, you are such a good person. I am so glad Eliana has found you," Lucy says.

We let go of each other to face everybody and Lucy has tears rolling down her cheeks.

"Aww, Aunt Lucy."

I get up to walk around the other side of the table. and hug her from behind.

"Eliana, ignore her. She's been like this a lot lately," Beth says.

Lucy dabs her eyes.

"Beth is right. Ignore me. Seeing you with Brent reminds me of when we were teens and the way Andy was with us," she explains.

The rest of the afternoon is spent talking with my Aunts and them grilling Brent about everything, until finally, Shane manages to pry them away to go home.

CHAPTER FIFTEEN

IT'S Brent's twenty-sixth birthday and I've decided to surprise him at work. I've only ever walked past the Stardust Hotel before. It's a cream building with touches of red stone. The steps leading up to the entrance are black. I glide my hand along the gold handrail at the side of the steps. It's all quite glamorous. The doorman smiles as I reach the top of the steps and holds the entrance door open for me.

"Thank you," I say as I walk into the hotel lobby carrying the blue gift bag.

There is a big, long desk to the left side of the lobby and the whole of the lobby is finished in cream marble. Leading off the lobby to the centre is a marble staircase, that splits at the middle leading to two more staircases with red carpets. I'm so mesmerised by it all and I find myself staring at the floating glass chandeliers.

"Oops, sorry." I apologise to a porter and she smiles.

"First time at the hotel?" she asks.

"Yeah. Actually, I'm looking for Brent," I explain. "Is he working today?"

"Yes he is. If you'd like to follow me to reception, I'll go grab him for you." She nods.

She leads me over to the reception area, then disappears for a few moments before returning with Brent. I can't help but be taken aback by how smart he looks in his uniform; black suit, white shirt and yellow tie.

"Hey, this is a nice surprise," he says as he makes his way around the reception desk to greet me.

I hold out his gift.

"I wanted to come and wish you happy birthday."

"Aww thanks, Eliana. You didn't have to..."

"Yes I did. Open it," I order.

He opens the bag and pulls out the bottle of Coolwater For Men.

"My favourite," he says beaming.

"You kept that quiet, Brent," the porter from earlier makes her way to him and kisses him on the cheek.

"Happy birthday."

"Thanks, Khloe."

Brent turns to me.

"This is my sister Eliana. Eli, this is Khloe," he makes the introduction.

"Nice to meet you, Eliana," Khloe says.

I shake her hand.

"You too. I'd better let you get back to work or you'll both be in trouble with your boss. I'll text you later, Brent."

I head out the doors and suddenly I hear him calling me.

"Just a sec, Eli."

Brent looks a little awkward.

"I just want to say thank you again and to ask if you can tell Beth and Lucy I said thank you for the cards and money?"

"Of course I will."

He shuffles.

"I really wasn't expecting anything. I've kind of got used to it being just like any other day."

"Well, you aren't on your own anymore, Brent," I tell him. "You have me, two aunts and a crazy cousin, who love you."

Now I blush.

"I would hug you but we are at your place of work." I add.

Brent laughs.

"Sod that, I don't care. You're my kid sister and if I want to hug you then I will."

He pulls me close and wraps his arms around me. His Hugo Boss aftershave smells lush, just then a car screeches nearby and a shout startles me.

"Get out of the car, bitch. You'll have to get a bus home later. I'm having a few of the guys over for a party."

We watch a small girl with dark, brown hair and uniform like Khloe's get out of the car. She rushes up the steps and into the hotel as the car races off.

Brent looks concerned.

"I'd better go check on Brooke."

I watch him disappear into the hotel and wonder if Brooke is the girl he likes.

CHAPTER SIXTEEN

AFTER dropping the present and cards off to Brent, I pop in to visit Shane. He still has issues with Alexis, as the girl just won't take no for an answer.

"Eliana, you're a girl," he says pacing the floor, "What can I do to get her to take the hint? I've blocked her on social media, but she gets her friends to message me. It's doing my head in. The crazy bitch is nuts."

"Alexis clearly thinks there is still a chance with you. The way I see it, the only thing that will give her the final hint is maybe show her you've moved on."

Shane sighs.

"How do you suggest I do that?"

I shrug.

"Maybe get her to think you're seeing somebody else."

"Oh yeah?"

"Yeah. Maybe get a friend to fake being your girlfriend," I laugh, "If you're desperate enough."

"Oh, I am definitely desperate enough. There's only so much of that crazy bitch I can take. It's got so bad, I was going to ask if I could move in with you."

I laugh again.

"It can't be that bad, surely?"

Suddenly Beth appears.

"Eliana, did you see Brent today?"

"Yeah and he said thank you for the cards. He wasn't expecting anything from us."

Beth sighs and shakes her head.

"That boy. We really ought to do something for his birthday."

"Such as?"

Beth looks thoughtful.

"Maybe throw him a party?" she suggests.

"That's an idea," Shane says.

"Yeah, I might see if I can get his flatmate to invite some of his friends too," I add.

"Aunt Beth, did you see mum?" Shane asks.

Beth laughs.

"Yes, we went to my house. She's outside talking to your old neighbour, Mr Brown," Beth explains as the front door opens and Lucy rushes in.

"Beth, I told you to wait for me, or he would keep me talking," she says breathlessly.

Beth narrows her eyes.

"Well, you don't need any encouragement. When you start, you could talk for hours." Beth replies laughing. Lucy rolls her eyes before she turns to me.

"Eliana, I wasn't expecting you to be here."

I smile and shrug.

"Well here I am, I guess."

"Is everything okay with Brent?" she asks.

"Yeah, I was just telling Aunt Beth, he said thanks for the birthday stuff. He really wasn't expecting anything from us."

"That boy. When will he realise he has family now?" she says.

Suddenly there is an urgent knock at the door, so Lucy answers it and we hear Alexis.

"Mrs Smith, is Shane at home? I really need to speak to him."

With the door ajar, she glances back at Shane, he shakes his head and mouths, 'No way.'

Lucy pulls the door in tightly.

"Alexis, you need to stop calling around here. After the way you attacked my god-daughter, I don't know how you have the nerve. Now if you don't mind, I have family round and I don't have time for your dramas." She shuts the door and Shane claps his hands.

"Mother, I applaud you. That girl has not left me alone. She's crazy and you just shut her down." He walks over to her and hugs her.

"Like I keep telling you," Lucy warns, "Pick better girlfriends."

"I know," Shane says. "But you know you love me, mam."

Lucy eyes him suspiciously.

"Why do I get the feeling something is brewing?"

Shane clears his throat.

"Mam, I want to move in with Eliana for a while."

My aunt gasps.

"Alexis doesn't know where she lives," Shane explains, "So I can escape from her until things blow over."

Lucy sinks down onto the sofa.

"It's a shock, I'll give you that, Shane."

She turns to face me.

"Eliana, is this okay with you? He's such a noisy, messy person."

I laugh and shake my head.

"No worries, I don't mind. It will be nice having somebody else in the house," I tell her.

Shane exhales.

"Now that's sorted, when can I move in?" he asks.

"Drop your stuff off later if you like," I say. "Actually Shane, can you come with me to Brent's place? I want to see if I can catch his flatmate at home, before he finishes work."

Shane agrees and heads off to his room to pack.

WE get off the bus and walk to the flat. I knock on the front door and it opens to a shirtless Owen and he smirks at me.

"Well look who it is. I just knew you wouldn't be able to resist my charms."

I make the introductions quickly.

"Owen, this is my cousin Shane. Shane, Owen."

Both nod.

"We wanted to talk to you about throwing a party for Brent's birthday tomorrow night," I inform Owen. "Maybe get some of his friends from work to come."

"Party, I like the sound of that," Owen says looking me up and down. "I'm not sure it's Brent's kind of thing though."

"Well if he doesn't, you can blame us," I assure him.

"Awesome," Owen says. "Would you like to come in or do you have somewhere you need to be?"

Shane steps forward.

"Actually, I need the bog."

"This way," Owen says, and we follow him.

"Toilet is through there," he says, pointing to the door.

"Thanks," Shane replies and rushes off closing the door behind him.

I walk into the living room and notice the television is paused on a dirty film and I turn away. Owen steps around me and grabs my waist.

"Fancy a movie?" he smirks.

Suddenly we hear the toilet flush and Owen turns off the TV as Shane steps out of the bathroom.

"Nice place you guys have," Shane remarks. "Shame you don't have a third bedroom."

"So, what do you want us to bring to the party?" I ask quickly. I barely look at Owen.

"Can you get two bottles of vodka and a case of beer?" Owen asks. "I'll get the rest."

"Yeah," Shane says. "We can do that, right Eli?"

I nod at Shane.

"Sure. Now let's get going, we can go for some supplies," I finally look at Owen. "Keep it a surprise for Brent. He deserves one night to blow out."

"Sure thing," Owen says as we leave.

"Jesus Eli, you fancy slowing down?" Shane asks.

"Sorry, I need to be somewhere after we get supplies," I lie.

I feel my face burn, Owen is turning into a real sleaze. Once our birthdays are done, I'm going to have a chat to Brent about him.

CHAPTER SEVENTEEN

TODAY is the day of the surprise party for Brent. I didn't want to give Owen my number, so I told Shane to give him his, instead of mine.

"Eli, I think you are just imagining that Owen is being flirty with you. He's probably just being friendly," Shane says.

"Shane, I'm deadly serious. He *is* flirting with me every chance he gets. I hope his girlfriend is here tonight. Maybe then, the slimeball will leave me alone," I say as we walk down the steps to Brent's flat.

I grab his arm and he turns to face me.

"Shane, do I look okay? I want to make a good impression on Brent's other friends."

The black skirt I'm wearing falls just above my knees and my white strappy top flows just over it.

"Eliana, you look amazing as always," Shane laughs. "But I don't know how you can walk in those heels."

"I can keep up the pace," I tell him as we finish the steps.

"Owen said Brent's work colleague text. She's taking Brent for a drink and is going to come up with a story to get him to come back here, so they shouldn't be too long," Shane says. "Are you sure you can make it in those heels?"

"I've got my flats in my bag anyway so if it gets too much I'll change them."

Suddenly there are voices coming from the street.

"That's Brent," I say.

We rush around the corner to the flat and knock on the door, before entering. Owen sticks his head around the corner at the top of the stairs.

"Talk about cutting it fine. Quick, he's at the gate with Khloe."

Owen offers his hand and I begrudgingly take it. Shane is right behind and Owen pushes us into his room. It's full of people. I glance into the kitchen to see that it is also full of before Owen dims the lights. He tells everybody to be quiet and hide just before the door opens. We hear Brent chatting innocently before he shouts.

"Owen, you still up? Khloe wanted to pop by to see you."

"Yeah, I'm in the bedroom," Owen answers.

"Surprise," we all shout as Brent turns on the light. The look on his face is priceless.

"I really wasn't expecting this. I can't believe you organised it all," he gushes. He looks at Owen and he shrugs.

"This wasn't my idea."

I step around Owen.

"It was my idea. I wanted to do something for you. It was your birthday yesterday and you deserve to party," I tell him and he wraps his arms around me in a bear hug.

"Thanks sis."

"Let's party," Owen shouts and someone turns on the music.

Brent is pulled away by some of his friends in a different direction. Owen is standing in front of me with a red-headed girl, wearing a short white dress.

"Eliana, this is Joanne," he turns and pecks Joanne on the cheek. "Gorgeous, this is Eliana, Brent's new sister."

Joanne fluffs her hair and smiles.

"Hey Eliana, it's nice to meet you." She turns to Owen and turns on a baby voice, "Babe, can you make me a cocktail?"

"Sure thing, sweetness," he answers and heads towards the kitchen.

"Owen," I shout and he glances back.

"Is it okay if I put my bag in one of the bedrooms?"

"Yeah sure thing, put it in Brent's room. I'll be busy with my woman later, so you won't be able to get it if it's in my room." He winks before walking off.

The party is in full swing and everybody is having a good time. Thankfully, Owen hasn't once tried to flirt with me since the wink. Maybe Shane is right about him.

THREE hours later, people begin to leave. Shane is wasted and making out with some girl in the corner. I hear Joanne from the other corner.

"Owen, you're a dick, I thought you loved me. Why won't you move in?"

"Baby, I do, but we've only been together six months. It's too soon to be thinking about that kind of stuff."

"Well screw you, I'm off to find another man who will really love me and not just want to be with me to get in my knickers," she yells and storms off and he races after her.

"She would be so much better without Owen. He's such a slime ball," I hear somebody say.

I walk out into the kitchen to get a drink, when I see Brent talking to the girl he went off to check on, when I surprised him at work. Brooke. She looks beautiful and happy, talking to him. She suddenly turns to me and moves away from him as he looks over at me.

"Hey sis, come here I want you to meet Brooke." I smile at her, and she lowers her eyes.

"Hey Brooke, I'm Eliana. Brent's little sister."

She looks up and smiles back.

"It's lovely to meet you." She shakes my hand. "Brent speaks so fondly of you at work."

I blush, then suddenly the phone in her bag starts ringing, so she excuses herself and answers it.

"Hello, just a second, mum."

She looks up at Brent.

"Is there somewhere quiet I can go to talk on the phone?"

"Yeah, follow me," Brent says and takes her to his bedroom.

I need some air so I step outside and nobody seems to notice me leave. I follow the path to the back of the flat to a small grass area with a small wall. A garden table is in the middle of the grass with two benches at either side. Owen is sitting on the one side, with a big bottle in front of him and I step forward, cautiously.

"Is everything okay, Owen?" I ask as I take a seat opposite. He glances at me before taking a swig from the bottle.

"Where did Joanne disappear to?"

He stares at me before he finally speaks.

"She's gone home, she's drunk," he tells me bluntly, before taking a big swig from the bottle.

"Okay, I guess you are not in the talkative mood."

As I stand up my heel gets stuck and I trip landing on my ass, making my skirt rise up my thighs. Owen rushes over and the smell of alcohol seems to be oozing out of him.

"You okay, sweetness?" he asks.

"Yeah, stupid heels." I reply as I feel his eyes on my legs.

"Let me help you up, gorgeous," he says holding his hand out to me.

I hesitate for a moment before accepting it. He gently pulls me up and I'm suddenly aware that our faces are inches away. Before I can react, his mouth is on mine. Remnants of the vodka he is drinking are on his lips. He tries to push his tongue inside my mouth and I muster as much strength as I can try to push him back, but he's holding me too tightly. Then I do the only thing I know will work, I bring my knee up and knee him between the legs. He releases me, moaning in pain and I give him a hard shove. He falls to the ground and I run off, leaving him there groaning. I rush up the steps but miss one and fall, grazing my leg. I manage to scramble back to my feet despite the pain and blood to go to the only place I feel safe; the castle gardens.

CHAPTER EIGHTEEN

AFTER running away from Owen, I manage to catch the late bus from around the corner. Luckily, I keep my bus pass inside my phone case. As I board the bus, the lady driver studies my leg and gives me some tissues to clean the blood.

It doesn't take long before the bus stops just outside the castle gardens. I thank the driver and step off the bus and head to the gardens as the bus drives away. There are a few drunk people over the road not paying attention to anything and wobbling all over the place. I climb up the gate and cock my leg over it, and a sharp pain shoots through it as I jump down to the other side. Thoughts of what happened with Owen hit me like a punch to the stomach. My heart feels like it's racing so fast, that it's going to jump out of my chest. My throat burns as I lean over to be sick all over the grass and tears begin to fall.

After a few moments when nothing else comes up, I use one of the tissues the driver gave me, to wipe my mouth. My head is pounding. I throw the tissue in the bin as I walk towards the bench and sit down on it and cover my face as reality sinks in. The tears fall hard and my body begins to tremble. It was meant to be a good night for my brother, but it's ended up being a disaster. Owen will probably never talk to me again and Brent will probably hate me for overreacting. Suddenly I feel sick again, so I lean forward and throw up. I wipe my mouth with the other side of the tissue, that I had used to wipe the blood off my knee, before I go back to the bench. Maybe if I stay here for a while, it will calm my stomach. I lie back and close my eyes, relieved by the cool breeze on my face.

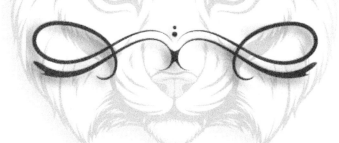

MY phone starts to rings and I open my eyes and glance around. Suddenly, I remember I'm in the castle gardens and grab my phone. It's Shane.

"Oh my God, Eliana. Where are you? Mum and Aunt Beth are going out of their minds. Brent is worried after his friend said he saw you running away from the party."

"You can tell them I'm fine. Where are you?" I ask.

"Still at Brent's. Where are you?"

"I woke up on the grass outside."

"What do you mean on the grass? You slept outside all night?"

I hear whispers in the background on the phone.

"Eliana, you're loudspeaker."

It's Brent.

"What happened? What's this about you sleeping on the grass? What grass?"

"Erm… the grass in my garden. I don't actually remember how I got here."

I pause and as I sit up, I see a giant stone Lynx facing me.

"What the…" I say as Shane cuts me off.

"Eliana, what's wrong? You're scaring us."

"Shane, can you come home? Quickly, please. My bag is in Brent's bedroom by the side of his bed. I don't have my keys or a coat."

"On my way." He says before he hangs up.

I look around.

What the hell happened to me last night?

I know I didn't drink that much.

I remember everything that happened with Owen and going to the gardens and then everything goes blank. I take my heels off, get off the grass and sit on the step by my front door. I stare at the stone Lynx sitting in the middle of the grass. The Lynx from the castle wall.

How on earth did it get here?

"Jesus, Eliana. You scared the crap out of us. Are you okay?" Shane asks as he walks up the path. Brent pays the taxi driver.

I nod.

"I'm fine. I have no idea how I got home or how," I point at the Lynx, "That got here."

Shane and Brent's eyes fall upon the Lynx.

"Did you take something you shouldn't have?" Shane asks with a disapproving look.

I roll my eyes.

"Drugs you mean? Shane really, I hate that kind of stuff…"

"Okay. I'm sorry." He cuts me off.

"Jesus, I stay away from people who deal in that kind of thing."

"Any ideas as to how that got here?" Brent asks.

I shrug.

"Anyway, how are *your* heads this morning?" I ask.

"No hangover," Shane says smugly.

"I went for a run this morning." Brent replies with a smile.

I lower my eyes.

"What about your flatmate?" I ask.

"Owen is Owen. Dying in bed so we left him there," Brent replies laughing. His eyes fall to the dried blood on my leg.

"What happened?"

"Jesus, Eliana." Shane says. "Come, let's get inside and get you cleaned up."

Shane opens the door with his key and I stand up and follow him inside.

"I'm going to have a shower and get cleaned up," I say hobbling. "Then, I'm going to go back to bed for a few hours."

I head upstairs before they start asking more questions.

C<small>HAPTER</small> N<small>INETEEN</small>

I'M still wondering how the stone Lynx ended up in my garden.

I mean, how did I manage to get from the castle garden to my own garden with the thing?

Nothing is making sense. I haven't heard from Owen, so I'm guessing he's blanked out. I have this weird feeling whenever I look out the window in the garden. It's like the green eyes on the Lynx are watching me.

I'm curled up staring at the television, when there is a knock at the door. I'm guessing it's Shane. He's left his key in his room before now, so I get up off the sofa to answer it. It's Owen and I try to close the door in his face, but he sticks his foot in the door to stop it.

"How did you find out my address?" I ask as I try to hide behind the door.

"I asked Shane." He says as he pushes the door open.

"Look, I came here to explain why I was being a dick at the party."

I stand guard. He isn't getting past.

"Joanne got under my skin, saying I wasn't man enough for her…"

I roll my eyes.

"And other stuff. You came out the wrong time I suppose. I saw red. You were gorgeous and seeing you in that skirt with your long legs on display, made me act like a horny teenager."

"Owen, either get to why you are here, or I'm going to call Brent and tell him exactly what you did to me."

Owen holds his hands up.

"Okay, okay. Look I'm sorry for what I did and I deserved the knee in the balls."

He pauses and gulps.

"And more, I suppose."

He looks down at his feet.

"Joanne texted. She's having our baby and she hates me."

I feel myself softening.

"It's karma I suppose. I just thought I'd come and apologise."

He looks at me before he leaves. I'm shocked. Maybe a leopard can change its spots after all.

WHEN the sky begins to turn dark, I decide to go back to the Castle gardens to see if there is a Lynx on the wall. As I approach the wall, I notice a space where it once sat. I blush realising what has happened. Yet, it doesn't make sense. The stone animals are meant to be fixed to the walls, and they weigh a ton. I cannot make sense of everything and before I realise it, I am climbing over the castle garden gate again. I sit on the bench like I usually do and gaze at the stars.

"Oh mum, what is happening to me? I must be losing my mind," I say gazing into the star-filled skies.

Suddenly I feel something touching my leg and I jump. It's a paw. I look down to see the cat-like creature.

"Hey big guy, where have you been?"

I smooth the cat's head and glance up to the sky, just in time to see a shooting star.

"Oh star so bright, shooting through the sky tonight, for my birthday, I wish you could help me find true happiness and a soulmate."

A lone tear falls as the star shoots by and I watch it slide down my face, before I look down at the cat.

"Well, big guy, I hope your master treats you right. If I could, I'd take you home with me tonight," I say before leaning forward to touch the animal.

I wrap my arms around its neck, rubbing my tears into its animal fur.

"Goodbye, my big guy. Maybe I'll see you soon," I say before I leave.

CHAPTER TWENTY

"HAPPY Birthday Eliana," Shane says as I come down the stairs. He's sitting on the sofa.

"This is for you. I hope you like it," he says holding out a gift bag.

"Thanks," I say, taking the gift bag.

I sit down beside him on the sofa, before I reach into the bag and pull out a small box. Inside the box, is a pair of silver heart, diamond earrings.

"Mum said they are your style," he says. "I asked her to come with me when I bought them."

"They're beautiful, Shane. Thank you so much."

I reach over to hug him.

"Mum thought you would prefer money so you can buy whatever you want," Shane says as he watches me open the cards from Aunt Lucy and Beth.

"Yeah she's right. I'm in the middle of saving for this gold locket I saw in town. I want to have photos of mum and dad in it, so that I can carry them around with me," I explain.

Later that morning, I catch up with my Aunts outside Stardust.

"Here's the birthday girl," Lucy shouts as she approaches and she hugs me.

"Happy birthday, sweetie," Beth says approaching from behind.

"Thanks, and thanks for the money," I say.

"Did Brent tell you what he has booked for you today?" Lucy asks.

I shake my head.

"Not really. The only thing he did say is that they have the new fish pedicure here in the pamper suite," I reply as we walk up the steps to the hotel entrance.

The doorman opens the door for us, and we walk in. Khloe is behind the reception desk and she smiles.

"Hello ladies, Brent told me he's booked you in for a pamper session. If, you would like to follow me I will take you up to the suite." She says as she comes out from behind the desk to lead us through.

"This place is so posh," Beth whispers.

Khloe takes us into a white room with soft cream sofas and two massage tables and nods towards an area marked private.

"If you ladies would like to change into the robes over there behind the curtains. You will start off with a back massage, followed by a fish pedicure," she explains.

"Thank you Khloe," I say.

"No worries. When you are changed just pop next door. Diane is waiting for you."

Once we are changed into the robes, I remember Khloe's instruction and head next door. Diane is in the corner, setting out the massage lotions.

"I'm here for the back massage," I explain.

Diane nods towards the massage table.

"If you would like to take off the robe and get up onto the table, stomach down," Diane explains.

I take off the robe and climb up onto the table. Diane places a blanket over the lower half of my body, before she starts rubbing my back. Before I know it, I fall asleep.

"Hey, Sleeping Beauty. Wakey, wakey."

Beth is shaking me.

I rub my eyes.

"Oh wow, I can't believe I actually fell asleep. I'm so sorry," I apologise.

Diane laughs.

"It happens a lot," she says before she leaves the room.

"Our fish pedicure is next," Lucy says excitedly.

It takes a few minutes for us to dress, before we are taken to another room. It has chairs lined up along the wall with fish tanks in front of them. A lady dressed in white, checks a clipboard.

"Hi, I'm Lily. Is this your first time having a fish pedicure?"

"Yeah actually, it is," I reply, not knowing what to expect.

"If you take off your shoes and socks, roll up your trousers and take a seat," she instructs me.

"Make sure you are sitting comfortably and then slowly ease your feet into the tanks," she goes on and I follow the instructions.

"Oh my. Dear Lord. That tickles so much," Lucy giggles.

"It's not that bad," I laugh, enjoying the sensation. "Does it harm the fish?" I ask.

Lily smiles.

"Oh no. They are fine, really. They eat the dead skin from your feet."

Lucy scrunches up her face.

"How does it feel?" Lily asks.

"Really good, actually."

"I have to agree with Eliana," Beth pipes up, "It feels so good."

"Good," Lily says. "Now if you would like to sit back, close your eyes and just relax."

We close our eyes. The little nibbling at my feet feels strange and I can't wait to tell Shane about Aunt Lucy.

"Eliana, are you laughing at me?" Lucy asks, still giggling.

"The noises you're making, Aunt Lucy, are so funny," I reply.

After a few moments the laughter dies down and I hear a door open and assume it is somebody else coming in for a treatment.

"Happy Birthday to you, happy birthday to you, happy birthday dear Eliana, happy birthday to you."

I open my eyes to see Brent and Shane holding a chocolate birthday cake.

"You guys." I say. "You shouldn't have. You're going to make me cry."

"Happy birthday, sis. Blow out the candles," Brent orders.

He leans towards me with the cake and I blow out the them out. Everybody cheers and I blush. Brent passes the cake to Shane who puts it on the counter.

"This is for you," he says, passing me a long navy rectangular box, with a bow on. I open the box and gasp. It's the locket I've been saving for.

"Brent, I can't believe you got me this. It costs so much," I say as the tears fall.

"Open it," he orders.

I unclasp the locket to find a photograph of mum and dad on their wedding day. I lift my feet out of the fish tank and jump over it to dash at Brent and wrap my arms around him.

"I really can't believe you have done all this for me," I cry, "We haven't known each other long and you have done more for me, than anyone my life. I love you Brent." I exclaim as I hug the life out of him.

"I love you too, Eliana. You're my little sister. You've only just come into my life, but it seems like you have always been here," he says tapping his chest where his heart is.

"Our family is whole again," Lucy blubbers.

"I am so proud of you both," Beth says. "Brent, you came into Eliana's life when she needed somebody and you have a special bond. I love you both."

Beth begins to cry.

"God, I'm in a room with a bunch of babies," Shane says and Beth clips him around the ear to the sound of our laughter.

CHAPTER TWENTY-ONE

I'VE been dreading today. Since mum and dad died, the only thing I've wanted to do for my birthday this year, is lock myself away in my room and let the day go by, but my aunts have other ideas.

They are always there for me, even when I don't expect them to be and Shane is more than just my cousin. He's more like the brother I've never had, until Brent came along. They have all made my day really special. If it wasn't for them, I wouldn't have even put my head outside the front door today.

Brent came into my life when I needed him the most and I think he feels the same. I've been well and truly spoilt today. After we are done in the pamper suite, we say goodbye to him, before Beth and Lucy take me shopping.

"I'll take that back to the house," Shane says lifting the birthday cake.

Everybody is so sweet.

IT'S late afternoon when we finally get home. When they promised to take me shopping, they weren't kidding; my legs feel as if they are going to drop off. I drop my bags on the floor and collapse on the settee, closing my eyes.

"You look exhausted. Mum and Aunt Beth are demons when they go shopping together. That's why I escape anytime they suggest going," I hear Shane laughing, as he comes down the stairs and I open my eyes and glance at him.

"Tell me about it, my feet are crying. I don't think I have the energy to make it up the stairs."

Shane comes over to join me on the settee.

"So, what are we doing tonight?" he asks.

"I'm thinking of wine and a Chinese, or maybe an Indian and Netflix," I reply.

"That's boring. How about a party and we get drunk?" he suggests.

"The only thing I want to do is veg out on the sofa with food and a nice bottle of wine. I'm not really in the mood for a party," I explain.

He gives me his pouty look.

"How about a compromise? What if we just invite Brent, Khloe, Owen and his girlfriend around, order food and have a few drinks?"

I'm not convinced.

"Nothing big," Shane goes on, "Just a few of us to celebrate your birthday. You celebrated with the oldies, now let's have some fun."

I laugh.

"You're lucky Aunt Beth and Lucy haven't heard you call them oldies. You'd get a clip across the head."

He pouts again.

"Okay, I give in. Just them though, nobody else please, Shane," I order.

He holds up his hands.

"Fine, I'll go make some calls. Go jump in the shower to wake yourself up," he instructs.

"I need a nap for a couple of hours first, then I'll have a shower." I sigh.

I ease myself off the settee and grab my shopping bags, before heading up the stairs and my room. I dump the bags in the middle of the floor, before closing the door and diving onto the bed head first and close my eyes.

Music playing loudly downstairs wakes me. I glance at the clock on my beside table and see it's nearly seven-thirty.

Wow. I must've been out cold.

Suddenly there is a knock on the door and it's Shane.

"Eliana, are you awake?"

"Yeah, I just woke."

The door opens wider.

"You sleep like the dead. I tried to wake you over an hour ago, but you didn't hear. Everyone is downstairs except Brent. He's gone to meet a girl at the bus stop," he explains.

"I'll have a quick wash and change, then I'll be down," I tell him.

"Don't take too long or I'll send Owen up to find you," he says before he closes the door.

Once he's gone, I dig through the bags I brought home and find the black dress I bought, with the white top to wear underneath. I place them on my bed before going into the bathroom to wash. Once, I'm done, I walk back into the room to change into my new clothes. I pull my bobble out of my hair, leaving it fall to my shoulders and brush it, before heading downstairs.

"She's alive," Owen says as he walks towards me with Joanne by his side.

"Happy birthday, Eliana. This is for you."

Owen gives me a card.

"Thanks."

I open it, and an Amazon gift card falls out.

"You shouldn't have," I say to Owen as there is a knock on the front door.

"I need to get that if you will excuse me," I say and go to answer the door. It's Brent and Brooke.

"Hey sis, you remember Brooke from my party right?" he asks.

"Yeah I do. Hi Brooke. It's nice to see you again."

Brooke holds out a gift bag.

"This is for you. Happy birthday."

"Thanks, Brooke."

I motion for them to come inside and close the door. I open the bag and there's a bottle of rosé wine and a card.

"I wasn't sure if you were a red, rose, or white wine kind of girl," Brooke says.

"I love rosé. Thank you for this, but you didn't need to buy me anything," I say and give her a hug.

"Do you know everybody?" I ask.

Brooke nods.

"Yeah. I remember everyone from the party."

We all fall into easy conversation as the night goes on. The food is delicious as always from the Chinese. After we've eaten Owen and Joanne leave. Shane and Khloe disappear to his room and Brooke heads to the bathroom.

"Eliana, while we are alone, I just want to tell you something," Brent says. "I know today must have been hard on you, what with it being the first birthday without your parents."

"It had to happen," I say gulping my wine.

"Well, I just want you to know that even though we grew up with different mothers, I want you to know I will always be grateful that you came into my life." Brent smiles. "I will always be there for you no matter what. We are family and I love you. I hope your birthday was everything you deserved to have."

My eyes fill with tears.

"I'm glad you are in my life Brent. I love you too."

I walk over to him and hug him, squeezing him tightly. He squeezes me back.

We hear a cough.

"Sorry to interrupt, but it's getting late so I need to go," Brooke says.

"Why don't you crash here?" I suggest. "I can sleep in my parent's room and you can have mine."

"Thanks, but I need to go home," Brooke explains.

"I'll call us a taxi." Brent says as he picks up his phone and he looks up at me.

"I need to go too, but I'll call you tomorrow, sis."

Once they are gone, I clean up the glasses and bottles. Just as I finish washing the glasses, there is a knock at the front door. I look at the clock, and it's nearly eleven.

Who on earth is calling this late?

I wipe my hands, before I walk from the kitchen to answer the door. When, I open it, I see there's nobody there. I look down to see a small box and a white envelope on the step.

Weird.

I glance up and down the street to see if there is anyone hiding, before I pick up the box and envelope. I pause for a moment when I notice the stone Lynx has gone.

"Strange," I mumble to myself, before going back inside and closing the door.

CHAPTER TWENTY-TWO

I open the envelope. Inside there is a letter.

Dear birthday girl,

You came into my life many nights ago. No matter how hard I tried to scare and threaten you, you kept coming back to the gardens. Over time, you have worn down the walls that I have built up for so many years. You have wormed your way into my stone-cold heart and by piece by piece, you have chipped away the stone. I've watched from a distance your pain and saw that you were ill. You made a wish upon a shooting star and now the time to reveal who I am, is here. As it's your birthday your wish will come true for one night. Come to the gardens before the stroke of midnight and I will reveal my true self. Hope you like your birthday present.

Your friend

I place the letter down on the seat beside me.

Is this a joke?

I open the box revealing white tissue paper. I pick the tissue paper up and underneath is a red crystal.

"Wow."

Khloe startles me.

"Who gave you that?" she asks, staring into the box. I don't know what to say.

I place the lid back on carefully and notice she is wearing Shane's t-shirt.

"Are you staying the night?" I ask.

"Yeah, if that's okay. I just came down to get some water."

"No worries," I say trying to focus. "There are glasses on the draining board."

"Are you okay?" she asks.

"I'm just going to pop out. If Shane asks, can you tell him so he doesn't worry?"

"Yeah, of course I will. Are you sure you're okay?"

I nod.

"Be careful if you are going out though?"

"I will, thanks Khloe," I say grabbing the letter and crystal before going upstairs for my bag and purse.

I put everything in my bag and ring for a taxi. Twenty minutes later, the taxi drops me off near the castle. Once the driver pulls off, I climb over the gate and slowly walk into the gardens. The leaves rustle in the darkness.

"Okay, I'm here. I have your letter and the crystal," I shout.

I wait a few minutes for a reply, before the cat-like creature appears. Slowly it approaches me and I crouch down as it comes closer.

"Hey big guy, I didn't think I'd be seeing you again," I say.

The creature rubs its head against my hand.

"You are really friendly tonight, aren't you?"

The cat backs away as the moon comes out from behind the clouds. It shines brightly illuminating the path and the cat whines, moving its head from side to side. I hear something and it sounds like bones creaking. The animal hunches over before falling to the floor and curls into a ball, falling onto its side on the path.

"What the…"

I want to move forward but I find myself rooted to the spot. The dark fur seems to shrink into the body of the animal to be replaced by what looks like human skin. I want to look away but I can't. I keep watching as the animal rolls around on the floor. I see four furry legs become two long, pale legs. The head tilts back and the ears shrink into it. I gasp at the white pointed teeth on display as they change shape. The black face has disappeared, to be replaced by the face of a man, with jet black hair and goatee and he stands up. On his wrists are dark thick bands, and he is naked. His perfectly toned body glistens in the moonlight while his green eyes open and gaze at me.

"Eliana," I hear him say before everything goes black.

I feel like I'm floating as my eyes slowly open. Glowing green eyes are staring down at me, as I push his body away, making him fall backwards. I scramble up to try and get away from him.

"Who… What are you?" I manage to stutter.

This cannot possibly be real.

It must be a dream.

I pinch myself.

He smiles. and his teeth shine under the moonlight.

"You're not dreaming, Eliana. What you just saw was real."

"Is this some sort of sick prank?"

He laughs a deep throaty growl.

"No prank. I really was just a cat, or to be more precise, a Lynx."

He pauses for a moment as if he is waiting for my response, but I can't form any words to speak. Everything really does feel like a dream.

He sighs.

"I was cursed in 1892 by an evil Witch. When the garden walls were being built, she turned me into a stone Lynx."

I suddenly find my voice.

"You are barking mad. You expect me to believe you are 128 years old? I don't know what I just saw, but it isn't real. For a start witches *do not* exist," I say hysterically. He approaches slowly and I move further away.

"I know this must be a lot for you to take in."

"Just back off."

He isn't giving in though.

"I'm technically 128 years old, but I was cursed when I was twenty-three," he explains as he stops in front of me.

My heart feels as if it's going to jump out of my chest. He reaches for my hands, slowly stepping forward.

"Look, I don't have a lot of time," he says quickly, "Once the clouds cover the moonlight, I change back into my Lynx form."

Something about the urgency of his voice convinces me, that this is definitely no prank.

"Why me? Why did you choose to reveal yourself to me?" I whisper and I notice that I haven't pushed his hand away.

"You made a wish on a shooting star for your birthday. That night when you cried, you shed a tear and it fell into my fur when you were hugging me in my Lynx form. Because of that, for one night the spell allowed me to reveal my true self."

He pauses and lets go of my right hand, before running his finger along my cheek.

"When someone wishes on a shooting star and sheds a tear, the tear becomes magical."

"So, I broke the spell?"

"You are the only person in a hundred and twenty-eight years to care about me in my Lynx form. You said if you could, you would take me home, because of that I was released from my curse for one night. You showed a caring side towards me in my animal form, so you are allowed to see me in human form."

"Why did you send me a crystal for my birthday?" I ask.

"Because after tonight, I will only be able to appear in my human form on the next full moon, unless I find true love," he explains.

He lets go of my other hand, before cupping my face with both of his.

"Eliana, I hope you find your true soulmate. You have been through so much pain and heartbreak. I would be cursed a million times more, if it meant I could find you again. Happy birthday and goodbye my sweet princess," he says and kisses me.

My eyes flutter close as I melt into him. Something deep inside me sparks and for a moment, all that exists is that kiss.

Suddenly I feel a cold breeze and I open my eyes and he's gone. I glance around the gardens but there is no sign of him. I touch my lips and gaze up into the sky. The moon is hidden behind the dark clouds. I walk across the garden to the bench on the floor and pick up the crystal. I cup it in my hand and close my eyes.

"Wherever you are, I want you to know you have touched my heart," I say into the darkness, before placing a kiss on the crystal.

"Goodbye my dark beast."

I glance back through the gardens but it is empty. I walk over to a bush to hide the crystal under it, before heading home.

CHAPTER TWENTY-THREE

IT'S been two weeks since my birthday. I haven't seen much of anybody. Brent is tied up with work, while Shane is loved up with Khloe, but it has been nice having him live with me. It's been a long time since there has been anyone else living in this house.

"Eliana, would you mind if Khloe stays over this weekend?"

I raise an eyebrow.

"We *are* dating now, you know."

"I kinda guessed that. No it's fine, I don't mind her staying over. She's your girlfriend and she's nice, not like Alexis. Have you heard anything else from her?" I ask him as our race on Mario Kart finishes.

"Yeah, mum said she has been banging the door practically every day to speak to me."

"What a psycho!"

Shane nods.

"Mum told her yesterday I had moved in with my new girlfriend," he smirks.

I burst into a giggle just as there is a knock on the door.

"I'll get it," he says, placing the Wii controller on the floor and jumps up off the sofa.

"Hey baby," I hear him drawl and Khloe comes in holding a box with a red ribbon.

"Hey Eliana, this was outside."

"Oh," I say getting up from the sofa.

I tear open the box to find a red crystal inside.

"Impossible," I mumble.

"It's beautiful," Khloe says. "You have another one now."

"Another what?" Shane asks striding over to see what is in the box.

"It's a crystal," Khloe pipes up. "Eliana had one the night of her birthday from a mystery admirer."

Shane eyes the crystal suspiciously.

"So, who is this mystery admirer?" he asks.

"I... don't know."

I hate lying but how can I explain?

How is this even possible?

I think back to that night. The Lynx, the man, the red crystal hidden in the bush.

"I need to go somewhere," I say more to myself than Shane. "I'm sure I'll be gone for the rest of the day."

"What's going on, Eliana?" His voice is barely audible amongst my thoughts.

"There is something I need to do," I say rushing to the stairs.

"Eliana, are you okay?" He calls.

"Yeah, you are kind of freaking out," Khloe adds.

"I'm just getting changed," I shout, pulling on a jumper.

I change the rest of my clothes frantically, before heading back downstairs.

"Keys, purse," I mumble searching.

"Kitchen worktop," Shane informs me and he follows me into the kitchen.

"What's all this about, cuz?"

"I'm fine, honestly," I assure him, "But there is somewhere I need to be." I rush out of the door, before he probes any further.

I get off my stop on the bus and run over to the castle gardens. It's still daylight, so the gate is open. There are people everywhere. I take out my phone to pretend to take photos near the bushes, hoping that the crystal is still where I put it, but it's gone. A little old woman walks up to me tapping me on the shoulder.

"Have you lost something dear?"

"Only my mind," I say.

She looks puzzled.

"Sorry. I thought I'd left something here," I explain.

The old lady is wearing a long brown skirt, with a cream blouse and long navy cardigan. A big battered brown bag with six pockets on it, is tucked protectively under her arm. I notice a green scarf covering her grey hair.

"What we lose will always find its way back to us," she mutters knowingly.

"That's good to know," I say.

"Even if we throw it away on purpose, with the intent on making it disappear," she mutters as she walks away.

I watch her walk off into the shadows. Suddenly a piece of paper falls from her bag and I run over, pick it up and call after her.

"Excuse me, you dropped this."

She turns around.

"Oh thank you dearie. You are too kind."

She takes the paper from me and I watch her stuff it back into her bag, before heading off. I sit on the bench for a while and soon the daylight fades and the skies turn dark. I look at the time on my phone and notice it's almost nine.

"You are still here I see?" a voice says.

I jump. I look up to see it's the little old lady. She walks right up to me, before sitting on the bench beside me.

"Are you okay?" I ask and she smiles.

"I am, but what about you, young lady? Did you find what you have been looking for after all this time?" she asks.

I shake my head.

"No. I didn't, but, what do you mean after all this time? Who are you?"

She laughs.

"You have a kind heart and a beautiful soul, my dear, but you don't pay much attention do you?"

I move slightly away from her as she drops the bag she's been clutching. and she stands and walks towards me.

"Listen, I don't know who you are but…" she cuts me off.

"My dear, I won't hurt you. I have been watching you visit these gardens a lot. Many years ago, I came across a young man. He was tall and handsome but as much as I was drawn to him, he just didn't like me, no matter how much I flirted with him," she laughs. "He was too busy flirting with other girls, so I did the only thing I could and cursed him."

She pauses and looks at me and I shrink back from her scrutiny.

"However, what I didn't account for was you. You see when I cursed Lynx, I turned him into a beast. It was the only way to make sure nobody would ever fall in love with him, or even care for him. What I didn't expect was you. You're so damn stubborn."

"I get it from my mother." I laugh shakily.

"He warned you to stay out of the gardens time after time, but you ignored the warnings, even when he revealed his beastly side," she tells me.

I get up ready to make my excuses to leave.

"But you cared for the beast. You even felt sorry for him, you shed that tear on his fur."

I glance at the gate and back at the woman standing in front of me.

"If you run away, you may never find the answers," she tells me.

"I do believe you have something that belongs to me," she says.

"I do?"

She holds out her hands.

"The crystal."

I take the crystal out of my pocket.

"You can have it. I'm leaving."

I put the crystal into her hand.

"You showed a caring side towards Lynx. That on top of that damn shooting star wish you made. That's how he was able to break the curse for a few moments on your birthday, to show you his true self."

Suddenly she reaches out, grabs my hand and stabs the pointed end of the crystal into the palm of my hand and drops of blood ooze out.

"Ouch, you crazy old bat, why did you do that?" I shout.

The moonlight shines from behind the clouds, half hidden, it gives off little light. Red sparks bounce off the crystal she's holding with drops of my blood.

"You've been lost for a long time, Eliana but now is the time to move forward with your life. You cared for him and now you can see him leave this earth for good," she tells me as the moon comes out from behind the clouds.

Suddenly a dark figure appears out of the shadows. It stops beside the old woman. It's Lynx and I gasp. He looks like a Greek God. The old woman takes out a blue crystal and puts it with the red one she already has.

"Lynx, I am setting you free from your curse. You have served your time," she says before driving the now bigger crystal with the sharp point on it through his chest.

I watch as he falls to the floor and disappears and freeze. My heart feels as if it has been pierced and tears begin to fall. I drop to my knees.

"Why did you have to kill him? You said you were setting him free."

"He has been set free my dear. Goodbye, Eliana," her voice fades before she vanishes.

Chapter Twenty-Four

I wake in the living room to the sound of the television in the background. I don't know how I made it home from the castle gardens, everything is a blur. I have no recollection of how I managed to get home. I feel numb.

She killed him right in front of me.

She lied to him.

She promised to set him free.

The tears begin to fall hard and fast, as keys jingle in the front door.

"Her face was priceless, Khloe. You are so bloody amazing. You managed to shut Alexis down in a space of five minutes and I've been trying for weeks to get her to leave me alone."

Shane and Khloe walk through the front door and he stops talking when he sees me on the sofa. He walks over as Khloe closes the front door.

"Hey," he says when he sees my tear stained cheeks.

"Eliana, what's wrong?"

Shane sits beside me on the edge of the sofa.

"I'll get a glass of water," Khloe says. and she rushes into the kitchen.

"She killed him, Shane. She killed Lynx in front of me." I say before breaking down.

"Khloe, call Brent. Tell him he needs to come here straight away," I hear him order as he rubs my back.

The image of her killing Lynx and him just standing there, not even fighting back, is imprinted in my head. Every time I close my eyes, I'm back in the castle gardens and it is happening over and over again.

Thirty minutes later, Brent arrives and I'm staring blankly into space, as the tears fall for Lynx.

"What is wrong with her?" Brent asks.

"I'm not sure," Shane explains. "She just keeps going on about someone killing Lynx."

"We can't seem to get through to her," Khloe says.

"Brent, do you think she has witnessed someone being murdered? Should we call the police?"

"Eliana, can you just explain what has happened?" Brent asks.

But I can only cry.

"Whoever it was, we may be able to track him down, Eliana," Shane points out.

Brent turns to Shane.

"Take Khloe home. Let me take care of Eliana. If I need to call the police, I will. I will call you later, but for now let's keep this between us. Don't mention it to Aunt Beth or Lucy, or anyone," Brent orders.

"Okay, I'll take Khloe home and come back…"

Brent cuts him off.

"You should stay with Khloe. I'm going to stay with Eliana and find out what's going on. I promise you now, I'm not going to leave her. She's my blood and I will do anything to protect her."

"Well just make sure you call me," Shane orders before he closes the front door.

Brent kneels down on the floor in front of the sofa.

"Eliana, what is going on?" he asks as he wipes the tears from my cheek and I look him in the eyes.

"She said she would set him free, Brent. She lied. She stabbed him," I half whisper the last words.

"Who, Eli? Who's stabbed somebody and who's been stabbed?"

I sit up slowly.

"The old woman. She killed Lynx and he just let her do it."

Brent looks at me sympathetically.

"Sis, it seems like you woke up from a bad dream you were having. No-one is dead. Everyone you love is here and your parents are looking down on you from above."

He leans forward and wraps his arms around me.

"Go have a shower, while I make you some food. We can watch a film," he suggests.

I do as he says.

Once I am out of the shower, I have some pasta. Before settling on my bed watching Mission Impossible Four, with Brent beside me.

"What we lose will always find its way back to us, even if we throw it away on purpose, with the intent on making it disappear."

My eyes open and I sit bolt upright in the bed. My heart is racing. Brent is sleeping beside me, still dressed in his uniform. I slowly ease myself off the bed and grab my fluffy dressing gown from the back of the door and swing it around my shoulders. I put my arms in one at a time and tie it up, before gently opening the bedroom door and sneaking out. I close it behind me quietly, trying not to wake him. I creep down the stairs and into the living room and turn on the table lamp, so I can see where I'm going. I walk over to the sofa, knowing my phone is there somewhere, feeling around the cushions. When I find it, I notice there are missed calls and a load of text messages. I walk over to the front door and open it, to go sit on the front step to gaze at the sky. I ignore my phone lighting up. Maybe I am losing my marbles and need to admit myself to a mental hospital.

Have I been imagining everything?

Maybe the grief from losing my parents has turned me into some kind of crazy person.

"Eliana, are you okay?"

I turn around to face Brent, his shirt is untucked and the top three buttons are undone.

"Did I wake you?" I ask and he shakes his head.

"No. Owen did. He was wondering if I would be back at the flat, straight after work."

Brent joins me on the step outside the front door. I glance at my phone and notice it's almost three in the morning.

"I'm sorry Shane had to call you. You probably think I am completely nuts."

"Eliana, you are my sister. I may not have grown up with you, but over the time I have spent with you, I have got to know you pretty well. I know for a fact you are not crazy."

"Really?"

"You haven't worked through the grief of losing your parents. It's because of that, you are having dreams."

Is Brent right?

Am I making things that don't exist appear?

"Have you spoken to anyone since your parents died?"

I shake my head.

"I don't want to talk about it. If they think I am crazy, they will put me on medication. I don't want to talk to some shrink."

"It might help. Doesn't have to be a shrink, I've got the number of a very good counsellor."

I shake my head again.

"Nah. I just need to find another way to deal with everything."

Brent turns to face me.

"Eliana, I love you okay? I hope you know that."

"I know, Brent, I love you too," I reply.

"Just maybe think about seeing somebody about these issues. Maybe speak to your doctor."

Suddenly a bolt of lightning from the sky hits the gate at the bottom of the garden path and it makes us jump.

"Woah. Where did that come from? Please tell me you saw that?" I ask.

"Yeah, I saw it. That was completely insane, I've never seen lightning up that close before."

We both stare at the sky.

"Brent…"

I pause as another bolt of lightning lights up the sky. It is followed by another one. This time it hits the grass, forming a big circle and it ignites in flames.

"Shit, call the fire brigade." Brent shouts.

The flames get higher and the heat coming from it is like an inferno.

"In the kitchen under the sink there is a small fire extinguisher," I say as I try to dial for emergency services.

My phone isn't working, Brent runs into the house and is back within seconds with the fire extinguisher. He aims it at the flames and they get smaller.

"Eliana, did you phone emergency services?" he asks as the flames slowly die out.

"Doesn't look like we need them," I say.

Heavy grey smoke surrounds us in the front garden.

"That was crazy," Brent states as he lowers the fire extinguisher and points at the grass.

"What is that?" he asks, glancing between me and the grass as the smoke falls away. He bends over coughing.

"What is it?" I ask.

My eyes burn from the smoke and his eyes widen as he looks back at me.

"What the fuck." he shouts, not believing whatever it is he can see.

CHAPTER TWENTY-FIVE

I walk over to Brent and grab onto him for support, as I cough. I squint my eyes, as the smoke is stinging them.

"Brent, what is it?"

I follow his eyes to try and see what he is staring at, but the smoke is too thick. There, in a circle of burnt grass on the ground, is a naked body curled up into a ball. I gasp as it moves.

"Go inside and call an ambulance," he shouts.

I don't move. I can't. I watch, glued to Brent's side as the body on the grass moves. Its curled up form straightens, as long legs stretch out. It sits up slowly before rising to its feet, stretching its arms above its head, before dropping them and slowly turning around. Two green eyes stare at me as the smoke clears. It's Lynx.

"But she killed you?" I mumble.

I let go of Brent and approach him and reach out and touch his face.

"I saw you die. Are you real or am I going crazy?" I whisper as tears fall. He smiles and cups my face into his hands.

"Does this feel real to you?" he asks before kissing me tenderly on the lips.

My eyes close. Everything goes dark. Suddenly, my body feels as if it is falling, but the ground never comes.

MY body is floating.

"My sweet angel, please come back to me," a voice calls.

"Eliana, wake up." I know that voice, it's Brent.

"Who the hell is he and why is he touching Eliana like that?" another voice shouts. It sounds like Shane.

My eyes flutter open and I find that I'm on the sofa. Brent is standing above me, trying to hold Shane back, as Lynx kneels over me, gently rubbing my cheek.

"My beautiful angel, you're awake. How do you feel?" he asks.

"Like I am dreaming," I whisper.

"Eliana you are awake. Are you alright?" Brent asks, I smile and nod.

"I'm fine."

I reach out to touch Lynx.

"Eliana, what the hell just happened?" Shane demands. "I tried calling you and Brent…"

"Everything's fine, Shane."

I slowly sit up.

"I will explain everything to you, I swear, but for now can you both give me and Lynx some space to talk."

Brent releases Shane and he takes a step towards Lynx.

"Please, Shane."

Shane scowls at Lynx.

"We will be in the kitchen sis, just shout if you need us," Brent says.

"Please tell me you are not serious about leaving her with him," Shane protests.

"I won't hurt Eliana," Lynx assures.

"Well, excuse me if I don't believe you, after the state she was earlier…"

"Shane, I am safe with Lynx. Give us some space, I will explain everything to you and Brent afterwards." I say as glance at Brent for support and he puts his arm around Shane.

"I don't know about you, but I could use a stiff drink," he suggests. Shane finally relents and goes with him into the kitchen.

Lynx gets up off the floor and sits beside me on the sofa.

"I thought that I was going crazy, that maybe I had imagined it all."

He reaches over and takes my hand in his.

"Eliana, you aren't going crazy. Everything you saw the other night was real."

"I don't understand. You just stood there and let that old woman kill you. Why didn't you run or fight back?" I ask.

"Do you remember what I told you on the night of your birthday?"

I nod.

"I was cursed by a Witch. Over the years the Witch came back to taunt me. The last time she came back, she said that she would change the curse. Soften it. I was able to walk at night in my animal form. She told me if I ever was lucky enough to find a girl, that showed no fear of me in my cat form, she would set me free. I have watched many young ladies pass as I sat on the castle walls. None wandered into my gardens until you came. I lost all hope of ever being human again, until I met you. You were not afraid of the darkness, or of the threats I made, as I tried to scare you."

"Stubborn. That's me," I say. "Please go on."

Lynx shuffles.

"You kept coming back night after night and it wasn't until the night you were sick, that I finally gave in. My walls crumbled and my heart thawed. I didn't care anymore that I would live out the rest of my life as a stone animal by day and a beast at night. You made me weak. That night when you were sick, you passed out on the bench, I prayed for the Witch to come to me. She did and I begged her to turn me into a human, so I could bring you home. She agreed but on one condition; as soon as I got you home, I'd be turned back into stone."

"So, it was *you* who brought me home?"

"Yes, it was me. I carried you in the darkness under the shadows of the city. When you woke up that morning, I was on the grass nearby in stone. The Witch could see how much you affected me, how much you mean to me, so she tested you."

"I don't understand."

"She sent you a letter, knowing that you were curious about the voice in the darkness, but you didn't run scared at the sight before you. Instead, you watched, your heart-breaking as you saw my pain. I could feel your empathy. That took the Witch completely by surprise. She has never witnessed anything like it for centuries and that's the reason she killed me."

I gasp but he goes on.

"The red crystal had your blood on it when she stabbed me and when our blood mixed, it bound us. She knew she had to end the curse. I would have to die, before I could be reborn."

He pauses and looks for my reaction.

"What do you mean, it bound us?"

"Your blood brought me back, Eliana," he replies.

I don't know what to say. This is all so much. So incredible. We sit in silence for a moment.

"I still don't understand it all. What happened to the Witch?" I ask.

Lynx smiles.

"She's gone. Once the curse was broken she died, and I was set free. Free forever to live my life how I should have done, before she cursed me all those years ago," he explains. "I'm sorry you had to see me die. If I could have saved you from all the heartache and pain, I would have."

"Lynx, I don't care. I would do it all again in a heartbeat, if it meant I could have you in my life again. All that matters now is you are here with me and I never want to lose you again."

I lean over to kiss him and he lets go of my hand and cups my face.

Suddenly the door opens.

"Ahem."

We break apart smiling, still gazing into each other's eyes.

"I guess there's some explaining to do," I say as Shane and Brent come into the living room, with bottles of bud in their hands.

"That would be nice, but how about you start by introducing us to the half-naked guy and why in the hell is he wearing my shorts?" Shane asks.

"Actually I gave them to him. When he appeared on the grass, he was naked, so I just grabbed them off the radiator," Brent explains and Shane glances between us all.

"The explanation is?"

I turn to face Shane and Brent.

"Okay, this is Lynx." I say. I turn to face Lynx. "Lynx, this is Shane and Brent, my cousin and brother," he rises from the sofa and steps forward.

"Nice to meet you both."

I spend the next thirty minutes explaining everything to Brent and Shane. By the time I finish, they are staring at Lynx in disbelief.

"I know everything seems a little crazy..." Lynx tries to explain.

"A little crazy?" Shane interrupts. "Are you on drugs or smoking some weird shit?"

"Shane, it's the truth and I want you both to know that I love Eliana with every fibre of my being."

Lynx takes my hand and kisses it.

"I think we should all go to bed," I say. "It's been a long day and I don't know about you guys, but I am exhausted."

"You guys go and get some shut-eye. I think I am going to have another drink before I crash," Shane replies.

"I'm with Shane, I think I need another drink to process everything and then I'll crash on the sofa, if you don't mind," Brent adds.

"It may be better if I leave," Lynx says.

"You're staying," I say.

I take his hand, ignoring the look on Shane and Brent's faces, as I lead him to the stairs.

CHAPTER TWENTY-SIX

I roll over from my right side onto my left side in the bed and open my eyes. He's still here. For some reason I had expected him to leave. His emerald green eyes gaze back at me and we are both smiling.

"Good morning, Angel." He says this as he cups my cheek before leaning forward and kissing me tenderly.

He leaves me breathless as he pulls me closer, running his hand up and down my arm. My skin breaks into goosebumps at his touch and I feel like I'm in a bubble, just us.

"I wish we could stay like this forever. Never leave this room," I whisper.

Lynx places kisses on my face.

"We don't want to need to leave this room. I would happily stay here with you for the rest of the day."

Suddenly there is a knock at the door.

"Eliana, can we come in?" Brent calls.

I roll my eyes and Lynx laughs.

"If you must," I shout back and giggle.

The bedroom door opens and Brent walks in, followed by Shane.

"Sorry if we woke you," Brent apologises.

"You guys look exhausted," I say.

"We were up most of the night," Shane explains.

"Talking," Brent goes on. "At first we weren't sure what to believe, but after seeing Lynx emerge from the fire, I believe everything you said last night, as crazy as it sounds."

Brent pauses for a moment and glances at Shane, who nods.

"We think it would be better to keep all this stuff between us."

"Eli, you know how protective mum and aunt Beth are. They'll have you in the nearest loony bin," Shane says.

"As far as everybody else is concerned, you two met on a night out in Cardiff," Brent suggests.

I sit up as Lynx rolls on to his back, with his hands behind his head to face them better.

"I know what you are both saying, so we will keep it between us," I agree, "But, what about Khloe? She was here when I had a complete meltdown, when I thought Lynx was dead."

"Shane has already spoken to her."

"Yeah. You had a bad nightmare and it terrified you," Shane explains. "Oh and mum and Beth were going to call in this morning, but I said we would go over later for lunch. You can introduce Lynx."

"I can't make it to lunch, because I have some stuff to sort out," Brent says.

I sit up.

"Oh no you don't. If I have to deal with a million questions over dinner, then you will both be there to support me. You can do whatever you need to do this morning and then meet back here. Then we can all catch a taxi over to Aunt Lucy's later." I order.

"Okay, you win," Brent says. "Just give me a few hours and I'll be back before dinner."

Shane smirks.

"Dinner is going to be so much fun today."

I throw off the covers and jump out of bed.

"I am so glad you find this amusing. Wait until I mention Khloe, you will be in the firing line for questions then."

Shane's eye falls to my banana pyjamas.

"Nice pj's. You wouldn't dare."

I laugh.

"Oh, I would. Now that you've made fun of my pyjamas, I definitely will. Actually, you had better go tell Aunt Lucy there is one more for dinner and invite Khloe."

I push him out of the room through the bedroom door and lock it. I lean against the door and gaze at Lynx and he smiles.

"Come back to bed, beautiful," he orders as he throws the covers off to reveal his muscle toned abs. They look good enough to eat.

"You look so good in my bed."

I walk over to him filled with lust. He sits up, swings his legs over the edge of the bed. His cock thick and hard, stands to attention in his shorts and he reaches out and pulls me towards him.

"And you, my beautiful sweet angel."

He turns my wrist over and places a kiss on my pulse, before kissing his way up my arm.

"You taste so sweet."

He pulls me on top of him. As he falls backwards, his cock pokes through his shorts and into my stomach. He rolls us over and kisses along my neck, making me surrender to him. Slowly, he moves down my body with feather-like kisses. He reaches up and pulls down my shorts and knickers. I lift my hips, and he pulls them the rest of the way down my legs and throws them to the floor. He slowly works his way back up, kissing my ankle and up along my legs until he reaches my core. My eyes close, as he explores my body. I grip the sheet below me, arching my back off the bed. As ecstasy takes over, my body shakes. Slowly, I release the sheets from my grasp.

"You taste so good," he says. before he kisses me on the lips.

CHAPTER TWENTY SEVEN

TWO YEARS LATER

"ELIANA, are you ready? Mum was having a

meltdown when I spoke to her earlier this morning, about the cooker not being big enough," Shane shouts from downstairs.

"Aunt Lucy always stresses at this time of year," I shout back. "Is Khloe coming for dinner, or is she working tonight?"

I head down the stairs.

"I'm picking her up later. Where's Lynx?" he asks.

Suddenly the front door opens and Lynx enters, carrying a small brown paper bag.

"Hey," he says to Shane, and they do that weird man hug.

Over the last two years Shane, Brent and Lynx have become really close.

"Hey gorgeous, do you want this now, or do you want me to put it in the cupboard?" he asks.

"Thanks. I'll put it in my bag," I reply and take the brown paper bag off him.

"So, what's in the bag?" Shane asks.

I glance at Lynx and he smiles.

"Ladies stuff," I lie, before I head into the kitchen to get my bag. I tuck the brown paper bag inside it beside my phone and purse. I go into the hallway and check myself in the mirror.

"I'm ready. Let's go."

I open the front door, and we all spill out of the house.

"I still can't believe you are driving, Shane."

"Why? I'm a good driver," he laughs.

"Just kidding." I say as I give my cousin a friendly punch.

"I just can't believe how much you have changed in the last few years."

Shane rolls his eyes.

"I mean it. Getting a job, passing your driving test and settling down with Khloe, I'm really proud of you."

He reaches out and we hug.

"Aww, Eli. You will make me cry if you keep up with all this mushy stuff."

Lynx coughs.

"Let's get going, or Lucy and Beth will be calling to see where we are." He says as he ruffles Shane's hair.

"*And* you have to pick Khloe up from work on the way."

"Let' roll," Shane says and skips over to the car, as Lynx leans into me.

"Are you nervous?" he whispers.

I nod.

"A little, but whatever happens we will be fine…"

He cuts me off with a kiss.

"I love you, baby," he confesses as we break apart and I cup his face with my free hand.

"I love you more, Lynx."

The car horn startles us.

"Hey lovebirds, get your arses in the car. Some of us have girlfriends to pick up," Shane calls from the driver's seat.

We both laugh and I make my way out to the car, as Lynx locks the front door.

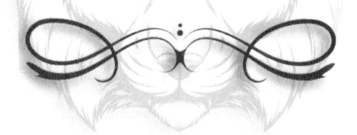

I T doesn't take us long to arrive at Aunt Lucy's house.

Brent's black Audi is parked outside. We jump out of the car and head into the house.

"Hello, Aunt Lucy?" I shout.

"In here," she shouts from the living room.

Brent is deep in conversation talking to Aunt Beth on the one sofa and Brooke is sitting in the armchair.

"Hi," I say hugging everyone.

"Wow Brooke, you are glowing. How do you feel?" I ask, glancing down at her baby bump.

"Like I am about to pop. I can't wait to hold this little one in my arms. It feels like he's on the go all of the time," she says.

"We've a little footballer in the making, growing in there," Brent says.

He sits on the arm of the armchair and rubs Brooke's baby bump.

"You two are so cute together," Lucy remarks. "You have been through so much, before finally getting together and now you have a baby on the way…"

Lucy is cut off by Shane.

"Mum, don't you start with the mushy stuff. I've already had to deal with it from Eliana and Lynx. They were like a couple of loved up teenagers…"

Beth cuts him off.

"You are one to talk about all the mushy stuff. I remember you being the same when you and Khloe first got together," she teases and we all laugh.

"Lucy, can I speak to you and Beth in the kitchen for a moment please?" Lynx asks.

I hope nobody notices my blush.

"Sure," Lucy says and the three of them go to the kitchen.

"I wonder what that's about," Shane asks.

"No idea. Brooke do you have any names yet for the baby?" I ask and she shakes her head.

"Not really, but there are a few we like. Adam, Noah, Luke, Lincoln, Wyatt and Taylor. I have been trying to convince Brent into liking Andy or Trey for a shorter version of Andrew, but he's not having it."

"I don't want to disrespect you Eliana," Brent says, "I know Andrew was our father, but for me, I just don't want to name my son after a man that didn't have anything to do with me as I grew up. The only good thing I have ever had from him was you."

"Aww Brent." I say and we hug.

"Who'd have thought looking through old letters would bring you into my life?" I say smiling.

"Do you ever regret that day we met, Eliana?" he asks.

"Never. You are my brother. You were a part of me that I never knew was missing, and I am so glad we found each other."

Brooke sniffs.

"Hey baby, what's wrong?" Brent asks.

"Nothing. Its happy tears, I swear. You two share a special bond and it makes me happy. Just ignore me, it's the hormones."

I crouch down to hug Brooke.

"Aww Brooke."

"That's enough mushy shit for one day," Shane says.

"Watch your language in my house, Shane," Lucy says entering the room.

"Aunt Lucy, where did Lynx and Beth go?" I ask.

"Beth forgot something, so she's gone back to her house and Lynx has gone to give her a hand. They shan't be long."

"I need to use the bathroom," I say.

I close the bathroom door and drop my bag on the floor. I take out the brown paper bag and empty the contents into my hand. Shaking, I flush the toilet and put the empty box and white stick on top of the wall cabinet, before I wash my hands.

"Eliana, how long are you going to be? I need wizz," Shane shouts from the other side of the bathroom door. I glance at the wall cabinet. It's high.

"Hold your horses," I say drying my hands.

When I open the door, he rushes in and heads to the toilet.

"Shane," I shout as I close the door.

"We're back," I hear Beth shout as I head down the stairs and walk into the living room.

"Did you find whatever you were looking for?" I ask.

Beth shakes her head.

"No, I didn't. I think I'm going to have the boys come over and go up my attic for me one day in the week."

Shane comes back into the living room and is ushered into the garden by Brent and Lynx. I sit with Brooke as Khloe goes to the bathroom.

"Eliana, while it's just us, I wanted to ask you something. I have already spoken to Brent and he agrees. You have been so good to me welcoming me into your family. You're like a sister, so I want to ask, will you be our son's godmother?"

"Of course, Brooke, I'd love to. Thank you for asking me."

Brent walks in amongst the hugging.

"Brooke's asked you then?" he asks as Shane and Lynx appear.

"I'm so honoured. Thank you both for asking me."

Brent hugs me.

"When we were talking about godparents for our son there was only one person we wanted. You are the perfect role model and if anything ever happened to either of us, you would make the best person to take care of our boy."

Lucy walks over to us.

"Anyone have something they would like to share?" she asks.

"Brent and Brooke have asked Eliana to be godmother," Shane says.

"What lovely news," Lucy gasps. "But does anybody else have news to share?"

Her eyes flit between Khloe and me as she reveals something she's hidden behind her back. It's a pregnancy test.

"So, which one of you are a mother to be?" she asks.

I gasp and drop to the sofa and Lynx rushes over dropping to his knees.

"You did the test?"

I nod, trying to process the news.

It's quiet.

"Lucy, let's give Eliana and Lynx some space. Shane, Khloe, Brent, Brooke, let's go into the kitchen," t Beth suggests.

"Angel, talk to me," Lynx says.

He cups my face with both of his hands and stares into my eyes. Tears start to fall. It slowly sinks in that I'm pregnant. I never thought it would happen because of what Lynx was before the curse was broken. He wipes my tears with his thumbs.

"Say something," Lynx presses. "How do you feel about this?"

I shrug.

"I never thought I'd get pregnant because of…"

I don't know how to say it. We have not spoken about it since the spell broke.

"Because of?"

I take a deep breath.

"Because of what you were before the curse," I whisper.

"So you're not happy?"

I grab his hands.

"I am so happy, I've got a part of both of us growing inside me. Something we've created from our love."

He smiles.

"You had me worried there. Let's go out into the garden for some air," he suggests.

He leads us outside and I close my eyes taking it all in, feeling the slight breeze in the air.

"Eliana, you know how much I love you right?" he asks. I open my eyes and stare at him and nod and he goes down onto one knee.

"I've never truly fallen in love with anyone until I met you. The moment I laid my eyes on you, I knew you would be the one to break the walls down, that I have built for centuries. You broke the stone around my heart and you saved me when I needed you most. I love you Eliana and I want to spend the rest of my life with you and our unborn child. Will you, Eliana Stevens, do the honour of becoming my wife?"

He opens a red velvet box, nestled in white cushion is a diamond ring, with a cut diamond in the centre surrounded by smaller ruby diamonds.

"My mother's ring." I gasp.

I haven't seen it since the day she died. I thought it had been buried with her.

"I don't know what to say," I reply.

"The usual response is yes or no," Shane shouts at the back door and I jump.

"Dude, seriously?" Lynx shouts back and the door closes as Lynx looks at me.

"So?"

"Lynx, I love you so much. I lost you once and it nearly broke me. I never want to feel that pain again. You make the pain I've held onto since my parents died, go away. You make me feel things I never thought possible. Yes I'll marry you."

He takes the ring out of the box and places it on my finger.

"You had me worried there," he says as he cups my face.

"I always knew I would say yes if you asked. It was the ring that took me by surprise. How did you get it?" I ask.

He smiles.

"Beth had the ring. Apparently it was in your mother's will, that when you found yourself in love with the right guy, she was to give it to him, to give to you. I spoke to Beth and Lucy earlier and asked for their permission to marry you. That was when they told me about your mother's request. I had every intention of asking you to be my wife. I had everything planned out in my head. Then you suspected you were pregnant and it made me scrap everything. Eliana Stevens, I love you with all of my heart and I can't wait to become a family with you and with this little one we created from love."

He drops down onto both knees and kisses my stomach, where our child is growing.

"I love you too, Lynx."

He stands and takes my hand.

"As much as I love being alone out here, I think we'd best go inside and face the music.

"Eliana, are you okay sis?" Brent asks as we enter the house and I smile at him.

"Yeah, everything is okay. I guess I have some explaining to do, huh?"

"Eliana, do you want to sit down?" Brent asks. He nods towards the empty seat beside Brooke, but I shake my head.

"I need to get this out."

I take a deep breath.

"I realised my period was late over the weekend and I asked Lynx to grab a test to see if I was just late, or pregnant. I did the test earlier when Shane rushed me. I was going to go back up and grab it but I didn't have a chance to get it before Aunt Lucy found it. I didn't know what the result was until she said..." I explain.

Lynx pulls me closer and wraps his arm around my waist.

"I'm so sorry it came out like that," Lucy says as she rushes over.

"How do you feel about becoming a mother?" Beth asks.

I glance at them all.

"I was shocked at first, but I am so happy. I can't wait to hold our little baby."

"I'm so proud of you sweetheart and your parents would be too." Lucy says as she squeezes me.

"Lucy, you need to let her go, she needs to breathe," Beth teases.

"Eli, can you tell us what we really want to know?" Shane asks. I smile.

"Of course I said yes. I love him."

I gaze up at Lynx.

"Okay, love birds, we have some celebrating to do. I'll go to the shops to get some bubbly," Shane says.

"I can't drink and neither can Brooke," I say as he heads for the door.

"Don't worry Eliana, I'll make sure he gets some non-alcoholic bubbles for you both," Khloe says following him.

It's then Beth picks up her bag.

"Eliana, there is something I found earlier when I went back to the house with Lynx. Brent, I think you should see this," Beth explains.

Her hand dips into her bag, and she pulls out a letter. Brent reads it over my shoulder.

My dear Eliana, if you are reading this, then I am no longer alive and your aunts have given you the engagement ring that your father bought me. I wish I could be there with you to celebrate your engagement and meet the man who has captured your heart. Whoever he is, he is a lucky guy.

You were our pride and joy when you were born. We fell hopelessly in love with you from the moment we first saw you. This may be hard for you to hear, baby girl, but you have a brother. Brent Carmichael. He is a few years older than you. If, you have a chance, you should find him. When Brent was small, I met him with his mother in a park. I recognised her from the photo she had sent to your dad, to tell him he had a son. She had no idea who I was. Brent was a beautiful boy, full of character. From the moment

I saw him, I knew he was your father's son, and I knew I not only had a daughter but a son too. Find each other before it's too late.

Love mum.

"Wow, mum knew about you," I say as I glance up at Brent.

"Yeah, and she called me her son, even though I'm not. She got her wish after all. We found each other and now you are stuck with me little sis." Brent smiles.

"I've decided to name our little boy Nicholas Andrew Carmichael. He won't have our father's name as a first name, but he can have it as a middle one," he whispers in my ear.

"Really?" I ask.

"Yeah. Do you think that will be okay?" Brent asks.

"It's perfect, Brent."

Suddenly the door opens and Shane and Khloe walk in carrying a few bottles.

"I'll go grab some glasses," Lucy says.

"I'll give you a hand," Beth adds.

They reappear moments later, carrying four glasses each. Shane and Khloe open the bottles, pour the bubbles and non-alcoholic bubbles into the glasses.

We raise our glasses.

"I just want to say thank you to everyone in this room for everything you have done for me. I finally have the family I have longed for, after losing both my parents and I have found love when I was least expecting it," I say, basking in the warmth of my family.

I lean in to kiss Lynx.

"You two need to get a room," Shane teases and everybody laughs.

"A toast to family and the future," Brent says, and we raise our glasses.

THE END

About Author

LM Evans discovered her love of romantic fiction and reading steamy romance novels. After reading Backstage pass by Olivia Cunning in 2011, soon after she started writing her own books. Publishing her debut book in 2014, since then she has gone to publish more books. She currently lives in South Wales with her husband, three children and crimson Rosella Boomerang.

Authors other titles

Starstruck

Unconditional

Sun, Sea and Boys

Tenerife Temptation

Coming soon

Forbidden fruit (To sir, with love)

Abs of steel series

Steamy story collection

Pumpkin princess

Stalker Links

Facebook
https://www.facebook.com/AUTHORL.MEVANS/

Twitter
https://twitter.com/Louisem07021983?s=09

Instagram
Louisem070283

Blog Facebook Page ~
https://www.facebook.com/BLOGLMEVANS

Blog ~
https://louisemarieevans.blogspot.co.uk/?m=1&zx=50bb660e29
3dfa01have

LYNX